You've Got Blackmail

NGTO

up in be   the used to be.   s, b. now works include more than 40 nction books on numerous subjects orical events, the arts, unexplained criminal investigation. She has never kmailed anyone . . . except, of course,

YOU've Got BlaCkMAIL

Rachel Wright

ff

faber and faber

First published in 2007
by Faber and Faber Limited
3 Queen Square London WCIN 3AU

Typeset by Faber and Faber Ltd
Printed in England by Mackays of Chatham plc, Kent

A CIP record for this book
is available from the British Library

ISBN 978-0-571-23515-5
ISBN 0-571-23515-8

For Elizabeth Sacre

Contents

1
The Madness Begins

I knew it was going to be a pants day when I woke up to the sound of Karen yelling. Karen's my older sister. She's seventeen and spectacularly annoying. She's also insanely secretive about every little thing she buys, which is why I'm forced to rummage through her stuff when she's out.

'Where's my new green nail polish?' she shouts, flinging open my bedroom door and barging in.

Honestly, what was the point of putting KEEP OUT KAREN on the door? I pull the duvet up round my ears.

'Oh, no, you don't!' she yells, yanking the cover clean off me.

I let out a yelp. 'What in the name of Nora are you doing?'

Karen has my duvet bunched tightly in both hands. Her eyes are narrow and her mouth pinched. It is not an attractive look, particularly for Karen who isn't what you'd call a stunner at the best of times.

'WHERE'S MY GREEN NAIL POLISH?'

'What green nail polish?' I reply supercool, even though Karen is breathing really hard through her nose.

'The green nail polish you obviously used to paint your toe nails.'

I look down at my toes. Oops!

'Oh, *that* green nail polish. I didn't realise you meant *that* green nail polish.'

By now a vein is throbbing in Karen's forehead. So I get up, to avoid getting thumped, and start rooting around under my bed, which is where I keep most of the stuff I don't want Karen or Mum to find. And as I pull out bags and mags and boxes and shoes, a bottle of emerald green nail polish rolls out from under the bed and across the floor.

'You are an arse, Lauren, do you know that?' snaps Karen snatching up the bottle. 'An absolute ARSE!'

And before I can say steady, she's out the door and down the stairs.

So, there I am sitting on the floor, knee-deep in bags, mags, boxes and stuff, wondering whether it's worth trying to shove everything back where it came from when something far under the bed catches my eye: a pink carrier bag from *A Cut Above*, which is the hair salon my mum runs on the High Street. I pull the bag towards me and look inside and my heart stops dead. Inside the bag are loads of stamped, type-addressed white envelopes, and inside the envelopes are invitations to a party at Mum's salon. I was supposed to have posted the invitations days ago. The party is tonight.

My heart is thumping like the clappers. Panic is rushing through my veins. What in the name of Nora am I going to *do*? If I phone Mum at the salon and tell her what I've done, I'll be grounded for eternity. And if I phone Dad, he'll tell me to come clean and own up to Mum.

I stare at the carrier bag like a complete idiot. Then I remember something: the *reason* Mum's having this party. The *reason* Mum's having this party is to thank all her regulars for using her salon (well, that, and to suck up to them before she puts up the prices). That means the invitations must be for her regular clients, and most of Mum's regulars live nearby. Ish.

Quickly, I tip the envelopes out of the bag and speed-read the address labels. Yesss! They're nearly all addressed to people who live round our way. Sort of. I glance at my alarm clock. *9.15* am. If I can get someone to drive me, I could have the invites delivered in loads of time for the party. But who to ask? The only person I know with a car who's free on Saturday morning is Karen, and naturally I'd rather stab myself in the eye with a rusty penknife than ask her for help, but:

1. These aren't natural times, and
2. I've lost my penknife.

I scoop the envelopes back into the carrier bag, grab Karen's street map from her desk drawer, bung the map into the bag, and bomb downstairs to find her sitting at the kitchen table painting her fingernails green.

'Hi,' I say. 'Nice colour.'

3

'Bog off, Lauren!'

So far, so normal.

I carry on, 'Could you give me a lift, please?'

The nail painting stops and Karen looks up at me, her mouth open like a goldfish.

'You are joking, aren't you?'

'It's an emergency.'

'What kind of emergency?'

'I need to deliver some stuff. It's really urgent.'

'What kind of stuff?'

'Er . . . invitations.'

'Invitations to what?'

Bloody Nora! If ever there's a shortage of police interrogators, Karen could fill in, no problem.

'Invitations to a party.'

'I hope you're not thinking of having a party here, Lauren. Mum's got enough on her plate at the moment without catering for some poxy party of yours as well as her own . . .' Karen breaks off, her eyes as big as gobstoppers. 'You didn't forget to post Mum's invitations, did you?'

'No! 'Course not. What kind of a plank do you take me for?'

Just then the doorbell goes and I shoot out of the kitchen to answer it.

It's Dave, Karen's boyfriend.

'Hi, Dave!' I say, grinning like a clown. 'She's in the kitchen.'

He looks at me blankly.

Good grief! 'Karen. The person you came to see. She's in the kitchen.'

4

I point towards the kitchen door.

'Ah!' he says, flashing me his sexy, laid-back smile.

And he strolls straight past me into the lounge.

Meanwhile, back at the front door, the bag of invitations is still clutched desperately in my hand. What I need is a cool, calm, sensible driver who won't go bonkersatronic when I tell them what I've done. Sadly, I don't know anyone like that, so I call Dex. Dex is my best mate. We've been friends ever since primary school. He's not like most of the boys in our Year. For one thing, he wears cool clothes and never gets into fights. And for another, you can have an intelligent and witty conversation with him about something other than football and poo.

I speed dial his number at home. (His mobile has just been nicked and his dad's being mean about buying him another one.) At last, he picks up.

'Dex, it's me!'

'Hey, Loz! Listen. I've got something vital to ask. If my life were a film, who'd you think should play me?'

'What?'

'I was thinking Orlando Bloom. Or maybe Johnny Depp, but when he was young, obviously.'

Orlando Bloom? Johnny Depp? What planet is the sad boy on?

'Look, Dex,' I tell him, 'much though I'd love to cast a horror film right now . . .' And before he can get a word in edgewise, I fill him in on the emergency so far.

'Bloody Nora!' he says when I'm finished. Then there is a pause while he has a think. Or at least I think he has a think – for all I know he's gone to Hollywood. Then he says, 'Here's what we do. We deliver the invites on our bikes.'

Now this sounds like a great idea to me except for one teeny, tiny detail.

'I don't have a bike.'

'No problemo. You can borrow Ed's.'

Ed is Dex's younger brother. He is ten years old and a freak. When he was eight, he announced that he wanted to be an assassin, and last month Dex found him drawing up plans for taking our school hostage.

'Brilliant! Thanks, Dex,' I reply in answer to his offer. 'I'll be over in a sec.' And quick as a wotsit, I'm washed, dressed, out the front door, down Park Road, along the High Street, and heading up Dex's street as fast as my size fives will carry me.

When I get to his house, I find him outside fiddling about with two bikes: one all gleaming chrome, fast and sleek; the other looking like it's not long been fished out of a canal.

'Nice bike!' I say, pointing at the one I'm guessing I'll be riding.

'Yeah, sorry about that. Ed doesn't do cleaning.'

As we stare at Ed's bike, a bit of rusty mudguard drops to the ground. Excellent. Now all I need is everyone I know to see me pedalling this clapped-out heap of crap and my day will be perfect.

'Right,' says Dex, scooting into his lounge. 'Here's the plan.'

'We've got a plan?'

'Of course, we've got a plan.'

Blimey!

Dex takes the carrier bag from my hand and tips the envelopes on to the floor.

'This is the plan. We divide the invites into two piles: one addressed to guests who live north and west of the High Street and one addressed to guests who live south and east. Then we take a pile each, get delivering, and meet back here. OK?'

The plan agreed, I squat down beside Dex and spread my street map out on the floor. He gets another map and two highlighter pens from a drawer, and we begin to divide the envelopes into a 'north/west' pile and a 'south/east' pile. As we divide, Dex highlights the roads 'north/west' on his map, and I copy him and mark the roads 'south/east' on my map. Then we put our piles of envelopes into separate carrier bags and head back to the bikes.

'Oh, by the way,' he says, balancing his carrier bag on his handlebars and swinging a leg over his crossbar, 'don't go up or down any hills if you can help it.'

'Why?'

'Because Ed's gears are knackered and his brakes don't work.'

Great. So no extra stress there, then.

★ ★ ★

It's almost three o'clock by the time I get back to Dex's house. My legs are shattered, my stomach is starving, and the soles of my groovy new sandals are wrecked from all that foot braking. I prop the so-called bike up against the wall, huff and puff up the steps to the front door and collapse on the bell. Ed answers.

'Is that my bike?' he asks, looking straight past me.

'Er . . . yeah. I was just, uh, checking it was safe.'

'That's a lie, isn't it, Lauren?'

'Yes, Ed. It is.'

Just then Dex appears from the kitchen waving a packet of Jaffa Cakes. Saved by a biscuit! I squeeze past Ed, giving him a shaky 'sorry' smile, and stagger into the kitchen, pull out a chair and sit down at the table, facing the door. If the little wacko is planning to assassinate me, I want to see him coming.

Over lunch – Jaffa Cakes, Ribena-milk, toast and a couple of grapes – Dex and I swop notes on Mission Invites. Turns out Dex has delivered all his invitations without being seen by anyone he knows. And I have delivered nearly all mine while being seen by practically *everyone* I know, including:

1. Lee Quick, who's in Year Ten and who all the girls have a super size crush on;
2. Mr Barnett, my English teacher, who looked through his net curtains just after I'd pushed his invite through his door.

I hate Mr Barnett. Of all the unreasonable teachers ever to be unreasonable, he is the unreasonablest. Listen to this for an example: last week, when we were doing *Antony and Cleopatra,* he asked me, Jez and Lee Bogie (yes, *really*) to read some of the play out loud. I was this old saddo called Enobarbus who rambles on about a boat he's seen Cleopatra sitting in. Anyway, this spellbinding (not) speech starts with the lines:

> The barge she sat in, like a burnish'd throne
> Burn'd upon the water.

But I got my tongue in a twist and said,

> The barge she *shat* in, like a burnish'd throne
> Burn'd upon the water.

That did it. Everyone lost it. Really lost it. In fact, Frank Fabiola laughed so hard, he fell off his chair and nearly knocked himself out. It was one of those moments of pure comedy genius that we all go to school for. But did Mr B crack his miserable face? Did he thank me for injecting some much-needed humour into the world's dullest play? No, he did not. Instead he gave me detention for, as he put it, being '. . . tiresomely immature yet again'.

The memory of Mr B's unreasonableness sets me off on one, and to calm me down, Dex reminds me of the time Mr B was invigilating an exam and it was totally quiet and he dropped his rubber on the floor, and when he bent over to pick it up, he farted. Like a foghorn. This happy, happy memory prompts Dex to sing *Wind Beneath My Wings,* and before long all stressy thoughts about Fartman Barnett and Mum's party are gone from my head, and me and Dex are howling with laughter. In fact, we're laughing so hard I almost don't hear my mobile ringing in the pocket of my combat shorts. I yank it out and push the button just in time.

'Hello?'

No answer.

I try again. 'Hello?'

Again no answer, although this time I can definitely hear someone breathing at the other end.

'Who is this?'

There is a long silence then a girl's voice comes on the line.

'You know who this is and you'd betta watch out, Lauren Cracknell, coz I'm gonna bust you up for what you did, and I'm gonna bust you up good.'

The line goes dead.

2
Bully Blancmange

The caller is right. I know exactly who she is. She's Tonya Ravonia, the meanest, nastiest, horriblest bully who ever lived. Tonya's in Year Nine like Dex and me. She's the size of a dump truck and so pale and blonde and blobby she looks like a giant vanilla blancmange. Yet underneath that puddingy exterior lurks pure vicious evil. When she was eleven, she used to chuck eggs at people's windows and wreck their gardens. Now she beats people up. Last term she cornered Jo Chandler alone in the loos and kicked her so hard, I can still hear Jo's scream. Of course, everyone knew what Tonya had done that day, but no one reported her. Not even Jo. We were all too scared of what she and her stick insect groupie, Fran Sharpe, might do in revenge.

My face must have gone the colour of ash or something during Tonya's call because as soon as I put down my phone Dex says, 'What's happened?'

I tell him about Tonya's threat and he practically chokes to death on a grape.

'*What* in the name of Phil Mitchell did you do to her?'

'Nothing! That's it! Nothing!'

I can feel my palms going clammy. I wipe them on my shorts and tell myself to stay calm. There's been some mistake. Which will get sorted. No need to freak out. No need to freak out! What am I *thinking*? There's a psycho mountain of blancmange out there waiting to get me!

'Tell you what,' says Dex, trying to sound all sensible and reassuring. 'I'll ring Nat, Tasha and Ems tonight to see if they know what Tonya's on about. Then we'll come up with a plan.'

I smile feebly and nod. Soon all my best pals will be on the case.

Oh. Dear. God.

I'm going to have to find my passport and leave the country.

Back home in my bedroom, getting ready for Mum's party, I think back over the day so far:

1. I've been caught borrowing Karen's stuff.
2. I've possibly ruined Mum's party.
3. A ten-year-old wacko may be after me.
4. A ten-tonne-wacko *is* after me.

Still, looking on the bright side, at least I managed to swipe Karen's new *Long Lash* mascara without her noticing.

I pull my hair back into a ponytail, layer on the mascara and glance at my alarm clock. 7.15 pm. Time to party! I say a quick prayer, 'Please, *please* God, let someone turn up besides Karen and me,' then charge downstairs to find her and Dave snogging on the sofa. Karen's lying back with her eye-linered eyes shut and her dyed black hair all fanned out like some Goth version of Sleeping Beauty (but without the Beauty bit, obviously) and Dave's got his hand up her T-shirt, although what he hopes to find up there is anyone's guess; Karen's boobs are smaller than two paracetamols on a surfboard. I tiptoe across to the sofa and shout, 'TIME TO CALL OFF THE SEARCH, DAVE' then leg it for the door.

The drive to the party takes ages, mainly because Karen insists on dropping Dave home. Via Honolulu. By the time we pull up outside Harper's Bookshop, which is across the street from the salon, I'm a bag of nerves.

'Hurry up, Big Bum,' snaps Karen irritably as I get out of the car.

I am just about to tell her where to go stick herself when I glance up at the bookshop and almost burst out of my skin. There in the window, larger than life, is a gigantic poster of Mr Barnett's face. And underneath his humungous bald head, in big black letters, it says:

HILARY BARNETT
Haunts of the Black-eyed Girl

And underneath that, handwritten on a separate bit of paper, it says:

I do not believe it! The world's most boring teacher has written a critically acclaimed novel?

I follow Karen across the street.

And his name's Hilary? *Hilary!*

YEEEEEEESSSSSSSSS!

I'm still grinning for England when I reach the salon. Once inside, I blow out a massive sigh of relief. It's *way* better than I could have hoped. There must be about fifteen people there already. Mum sees Karen and me and comes hurrying over.

'Girls!' she beams, giving us each a hug, 'so glad you're here.'

She looks really glam in her new silver sequinned top, black satin trousers and sky high, strappy silver sandals.

Karen says, 'You look fab, Mum. *Loads* slimmer. Weight Watchers is really paying off.'

'Ah!' says Mum, looking shifty. Then in a hushed voice she adds, 'It's not just Weight Watchers. It's also those magic slimming knickers I bought on Tuesday. You remember, Loz?'

Remember? How could I possibly forget? The experience has scarred me for life. We were in M&S. Mum was in the underwear bit; I was by the makeup when she held up these elasticated slimming knickers that looked

14

like a pair of old ladies' running shorts and, at the top of
her voice, yelled, 'Look, Loz! Slimming knicks!' Then,
when I stared over at her, horrified, she laughed hyster-
ically like she'd just made the funniest joke on Earth.

By now a small crowd has gathered to discuss the
wonder of Mum's miracle pantaloons, so I slope off to
chat to Christelle. Christelle is Mum's senior stylist.
She's twenty-two, really chatty, really pretty, really funny,
really French. Mum says she can be really fiery too, but
mercifully she's never been fiery with me. Christelle's
worked for Mum ever since the salon opened, but I
only got to know her properly last November when she
came to stay with us for a bit after her flatmate, Mercedes, was killed in a car crash. Mum was upset when
Mercedes died – she'd known her from this creative
writing course they'd done together – but Christelle
was heartbroken. Really heartbroken. Even though she
and Mercedes were totally different – for a start, Mercedes was spectacularly unstylish and deeply dippy –
they were Super Glue close. Mercedes didn't have any
relatives and Christelle had left Paris at sixteen to get
away from hers, so the two of them were like sisters to
each other.

But not like Karen and me are sisters to each other,
obviously.

I say, 'Hi Christelle. Like your hair.'

She frowns at herself in one of the mirrors. 'I am not
good for zis red colour,' she says to her reflection. 'For
me, it is not possible. Tomorrow, I change it, yes?' And
she flashes me her grin.

Christelle is forever changing her look and style. She says it's because she's French and in France they are very free (whatever that means) but I tell her it's because in her last life she was a chameleon.

After a bit of crucial hair talk, Christelle and I get stuck into one of our usual brainy debates: Tie-dye clothing, what is the point? And while we're busy chatting and giggling, Mum nips over, wine glass in hand, to ask Christelle if she's finished with the copy of *Haunts of the Black-eyed Girl* that she lent her, and can she bring it to work on Monday so that Cathy (the salon's cleaner) can have a borrow. At this Christelle says, 'Yes, OK.' And Mum, who isn't even looking at her because she's too busy waving to a tall tweedy woman across the room, says, 'Thanks, love,' and scoots off to join the Giant Tweed.

I eyeball Christelle in disbelief. 'You read a book?'

She smiles weakly. The last I heard, Christelle's greatest claim to fame was she'd only read one novel since leaving school and even that she hadn't finished.

'Your Mum recommended it,' she says.

I say, 'You do know it was written by my English teacher, don't you?'

Again she smiles vaguely. Then, gazing across the room, she mumbles, 'Yes, I know.'

While Christelle's brain is off somewhere else, Lucy and Kelly pass behind us, deep in conversation. As they go by, I catch a snatch of Kelly moaning about how broke she is (which is no major revelation as, according to Mum, Kelly never seems to have any dosh) and Lucy replies, 'Me too, and I've got a huge credit card bill to pay.'

I like Lucy. She's Mum's junior stylist. She's twenty-one, really friendly, really blonde, really sweet. Kelly is Mum's receptionist. She's eighteen, looks like Christina Aguilera – only with thicker makeup – and is unbelievably dense.

Catching my eye, Christelle half whispers, 'Guess what Kelly ask me today?'

'Go on.'

'Today she ask me, is America ze capital of ze USA?'

I laugh. 'What did you say?'

'I say, "I zink I want to stop talking to you now, Kelly", and I go into ze back room.'

Just then Karen marches over and announces that Mum wants me and her to pass round the snacks. So I wish Christelle a *bon voyage* and start circulating the vol au vents. And the cocktail sausages. And the mini quiches. And the Pringles. And the emergency bag of MilkyWays that Mum keeps for kids who hate having their hair cut. And while I'm slaving away, for no wages whatsoever, I overhear my mate Tasha's mum telling Cathy something that makes my ears stick out on stalks. Apparently, last night Tasha's dad went bonkersatronic and smashed up their new cordless phone! It was 11.45 pm; Tasha was in her room on the phone to Gary (her boyfriend) when her dad barged in. He snatched the phone from her hand and hurled it against the wall. Then he scooped it up off the floor and chucked it again, down the stairs.

Cathy gasps, 'Holy Mother of God! Why did he over-act like that?'

Tasha's mum sighs. 'Well, he doesn't like Gary very much. He thinks, at sixteen, he's too old for Natasha. And he's not happy that he can't hold down a job.'

The second I hear this, I snap into action. I dump the bag of Milky Ways in the rubber plant, whip my mobile out from the waistband of my jeans, and start to send Tasha a text. But no sooner have I punched in, *Wots wth ur dad?* than I hear a familiar voice bellowing my name. I turn round and, sure enough, it's Mum's mate, Man-mad Marge, over by the window – a pint of gin in one hand, a fag in the other. Reluctantly, I go over.

'Lauren, darling,' she shouts, swaying ever so slightly. 'I've just been checking out that tempting English teacher of yours.'

At the word 'tempting', she jabs a long red fingernail at the poster in the bookshop window opposite. I smile politely, but inside my head I'm going, *Tempting? Him? Only if you're wearing gin goggles, you man-mad goon.*

Man-mad Marge burbles on, slurring her words.

'Now, I know it's not easy with your mum and dad just getting separated and all that.'

She takes a long drag on her cigarette.

'But your mum needs to get on with her life and have a bit of fun, and that means she needs to find a man. And let's face it, darling . . .'

She slugs back another gulp of gin.

'Hilary is a catch . . .'

Huh?

'And he fancies her.'

'*WHAT?*'

'Of course he does. You remember how he used to drive her home after those creative-writing evening classes last summer?'

My stomach feels like it's going down too fast in a lift. There are prickles of panic all over my skin. What in the name of Nora is she *saying*? I force myself to think straight. OK, so Mr B used to drive Mum home after her evening class last summer, but so what? That doesn't mean anything. It was only because he taught the class, and our house is on his way home from the Sixth Form College, and Dad needed our car for cricket practice.

Man-mad Marge pours more gin down her throat and slurs on.

'Of course, your mum never got up to anything with Hilary back then . . .'

Nghh!

'She was still with your dad. Oh, and Hilary's wife was still on the scene. But now she's a free agent, it's time she got out there and started dating again . . .'

No!

'And Hilary Barnett is just the man for the job . . .'

Nooooo!

'Are you all right, love?' asks Mum, suddenly appearing beside me.

I want to yell, HOW CAN I BE ALL RIGHT WITH YOU ABOUT TO DO-THE-DO WITH FARTMAN BARNETT? But I just nod my head, lips pressed tight, then mumble something about needing fresh air.

Outside the salon, I speed dial Dex's number at home.

Ed answers. 'Yes?'

'Can I speak to Dex?'

There is a pause. Then Ed says in his weird flat voice, 'I told my mum about you taking my bike.'

Holy Moley! I click off my phone and redial. This time Dex picks up. Mercifully.

'Dex?'

'Yes.'

'I need to talk.'

'Oh, you've heard then.'

'What do you mean, "Oh, I've heard then"?'

'About the Tonya thing.'

'What about the Tonya thing?'

'You mean you haven't heard?'

'Haven't heard what?'

'About the Tonya thing.'

'DEX!'

'What?'

'You've got five seconds to start telling me about the Tonya thing and your time starts . . . now.'

3
Nightmare in a Nightie

Dex begins, 'I was on the phone to Tasha about who would play us all in the film of our lives. We reckoned Kelly Osbourne for you but without the drag queen makeup and . . .'

'Dex.'

'Yes?'

'Five seconds.'

'Oh, yeah, right. So, I was telling her about that picture you put together on the computer, the one of Tonya's head emerging from the back-end of a horse . . .'

I start laughing.

'And she started laughing and said when she saw it she nearly wet herself and what were you *thinking* sending it to the entire class.'

I stop laughing. '*WHAT?!*'

'That's what I said. Then it hit me.'

'What hit you?'

'What must've happened! Keep up, Loz. Remember I emailed the whole class yesterday about Mrs Goodheart's leaving present?'

'Yes.' Dex can be a bit tragic at times.

'Well, that's when you emailed me Tonya's picture, in reply to my email. But instead of pressing *Reply*, you must've pressed *Reply All*. That's why the whole class has seen Tonya's picture.'

I can feel my legs turning to rubber.

'Dex?' I quiver.

'Yes?'

'Tonya's going to beat me to a right pulp, isn't she?'

'Um . . . er . . . Possibly. Yes.'

★ ★ ★

Later that night, back home in bed, I wake up in an ice cold sweat.

Kelly Osbourne?!

Just because I've got thick, dark hair and womanly curves, and I dyed my fringe pink *once*!

★ ★ ★

Next morning (Sunday), I wake up full of the joys of summer . . . NOT. There is a knock at my door and Mum breezes in.

'Morning, Loz,' she chirps.

I poke my head out from under the duvet and scowl. Mum goes over to the window and opens the curtains. A blast of sunlight smacks me in the eyes. Excellent. Blindness. Just what I need to take my mind off my stresses.

Mum carries on, 'I'm off to church and then on to the supermarket, but I'll be back in plenty of time to drive you over to Dad's for lunch. Make sure you do your chores while I'm out.'

Dad's just moved into a flat in town, not far from my school. As a house-warming pressie I've got him these two small wind-up plastic nuns that you race across the floor. That should really cheer him up.

'OK,' I mumble in reply to Mum, and half an hour later I shuffle downstairs for that all-important first meal of the day: Jaffa Cakes and a cup of tea – except there are no Jaffa Cakes left since Mum blitzed the house of anything tasty, so I have to have a bowl of sugar-free cardboard, i.e. slimmers' cereal, instead.

While I chomp and chew, chomp and chew, I have a quick think about all the things I need to do to get my life sorted. (See, I am a mature person, despite what some may say – without naming names – well, Hilary Barnett, obviously.)

This is my plan:

1. Suss out Mum about the Hilary situation.
2. Arrange backup with mates to avoid a major duffing up by Tonya at school.
3. Do Friday's homework.
4. Do Thursday's homework.
5. Do chores.
6. See if Karen has got this month's *Chic*.

Now, as it turns out, Karen *has* got this month's *Chic*, and since she's 'working' at Pizza Heaven, I naturally take the opportunity to read it. Which means I haven't started my chores when Mum gets back. Which means she goes into a right one. Which means I have to delay Operation Suss-out until she's calmed down. Which means we're halfway to Dad's before I dare open my mouth! Luckily, I've watched quite a few episodes of the *Trisha* chat show, so I know a thing or two about quick, to-the-point interviewing. The secret is to start off all matey, to get your guest nice and relaxed, then put the boot in. I begin casually.

'Hello, Mum. Welcome to the show.'

She bursts out laughing. 'Thank you for having me.'

I roll my eyes. On *Trisha* the guests never say that. I carry on anyway.

'How's your creative-writing going?'

Mum shoots me a curious look. 'It's not, unfortunately. I never seem to find the time to get down to it. Shame really because I was so keen after those evening classes last summer. Your Mr Barnett is such an intelligent man.'

What?

'So interesting!'

HUH?

'As for Mercedes – God rest her soul – she was a revelation. We used to sit next to each other in class and once, when she went to the toilet I had a peek at this piece she'd been writing for classwork and it was *wonderful*: dream-like, moving, sad . . .'

I look at Mum, stunned.

'Puzzling, *very* polished . . .'

At this rate we could be here for days.

'She wrote on her grandfather's typewriter for inspiration, you know. He'd been a famous journalist in . . .'

Time to put the boot in. 'Mum, do you fancy Mr . . .?'

But before I can finish asking, this happens: there's some shocking swearing (not from me!), a screech of brakes and next thing, *Yikes!* We're doing a heart-stopping U-turn in the middle of the road and jerking to a stop outside a block of flats.

'This is it,' says Mum, slapping on a smile. 'Top floor. Flat 10.'

I rub my neck to ease the whiplash and look up at the dreary five-storey brick block.

'Aren't you coming in to say hello?' I ask.

There is a pause – a really long one. Then Mum says in a wobbly voice, 'Next time, eh?'

And I have to pinch myself hard to stop my eyes prickling.

★ ★ ★

For some reason the main door to Dad's block isn't properly closed, so I let myself into the communal foyer, which is bare and lonely: the paint on the walls is scratched, bits of the ceiling are flaking, and the lino on the floor is scuffed. I know the sensible thing is to blank this out, so I put my head down and charge up the stairs. When I get to the top, I lean on Dad's bell and instantly his door flings open.

'It's my little Lozenge!' he cries, giving me the biggest hug in the history of hugs. 'Come in, come in!'

Inside, the flat's not as depressing as I'd been dreading. There's a smell of roast lamb coming from the kitchen, which has a metal fire escape outside the window; in the hallway there's this brilliant framed poster of *The Clash,* which shows one of the band smashing up his guitar; and in the bedroom by Dad's bed, there's an enormous fake fur rug that looks like a flattened out tiger with a 3D head.

I point to the rug. 'A present from Uncle Nigel by any chance?'

Dad sighs. 'It's great on the feet when you get out of bed, but bloody unsettling if you step on the head.'

Mercifully, the lounge isn't too desperate, either. At one end, there's a big glass patio type door that leads on to a small balcony. Opposite the telly, there's a brand new bright blue sofabed, spoilt only by Dad's Whitcombe Wanderers' football scarf draped across the back of it. And on the stack of shelves next to the hi-fi, there's one of those glittery lava lamps that looks really funky in the dark. Also on the shelves, next to Dad's vast (not) collection of books, is a silver-framed photo of the four of us – him, Mum, Karen and me – laughing away on holiday.

Looking at the photo, I can feel my eyes prickling again. Dad gives me one of his hefty squeezes.

'Is this for me?' he asks, reaching for the gift-wrapped toy nuns in my hand.

I nod, he rips off the wrapping paper, and his face cracks into a grin.

'Never let it be said your old Dad's not an intellectual, eh?'

Just then the oven pings and Dad goes off to serve up while I lay the table on the balcony. Then, being a nosey kind of person, which I am, I lean over the rail to check out the balcony below. From what I can see, which is quite a bit because it sticks out much further than Dad's, it's kitted out like any other balcony except fixed to its wall there's this huge long window box. And inside the window box is a big tortoise with the name *Speedy Gonzalez* painted across its shell in white.

Now normally I'd just think: Hey, a tortoise, and that would be that. But for some bizarre reason, I want Dad to come see. So I go get him and we both go out onto the balcony and peer over the edge.

And there standing below us, beside the window box, is Tonya Ravonia.

Wearing a pink baby-doll nightie.

4

Operation Backup

I jump back about a metre from the edge of the balcony and stand with my jaw dropped open. I do not believe it! Out of all the people in the universe, the *Ravonias* have to be Dad's downstairs neighbours!

I signal for Dad to get inside quick and slam the balcony door shut behind him.

'What's the matter?' he asks, clearly confused. 'I know seeing a girl that size in a tiny nightie isn't easy but . . .'

'You've got to move flat.'

'*What?*'

'You can't carry on living here.'

'Steady on, Loz! I've only just moved in!'

My brain is now flipping out. There are so many thoughts crashing about in it, it's a wonder my head doesn't explode.

'Don't you see?' I say frantically. 'That girl is *Tonya Ravonia.*'

'I know.'

For a second I stare at Dad like a goldfish that's just been told it'll be sharing its bowl with a shark.

'You *know* her?'

'No, not personally, but her mum knocked on my door the day I moved in and Tonya's name was mentioned.'

I flop down on to the sofabed in sheer disbelief, thinking: Well, isn't *that* fab! Dad and Mrs Ravonia are the best of pals and Mum's practically doing-the-do with Mr B. I may as well kill myself now and save Tonya the bother.

'Tell you what,' says Dad like nothing has happened. 'Let's have some lunch and you can tell me what's up with you and Tonya and I'll tell you about my chat with Tracey.'

Over lunch on our laps in the lounge – which is, I have to say, a bit uncomfortable, what with it being 100°C with the balcony door shut in case the Blancmange is earwigging – I tell Dad about Tonya and her threat. At first he sits there quietly, nodding, listening. Then he gets all het up and starts saying it's about time he had a word with the Ravonias and Old Retardo (Mr Leonardo, my headteacher). Now, this is the last thing I want, obviously. I mean, if Tonya found out I'd split on her she'd kill me, *seriously*, and would probably knobble Dad too. It takes me for ever to make him promise not to tell anyone else what I've told him without my full permission . . . in writing.

The deal done – at last – Dad fills me in on his chat with Tracey. Turns out she and her husband and a couple of other people in the flats have got their knickers in a twist about the mobile phone mast on top of the block. She knocked on Dad's door because she wanted to persuade him to support their cause at a meeting at the Avondale Community Hall on Friday. Apparently, someone from the Council will be there. So will someone from the mobile phone company and someone from our local paper, *The Echo*.

'How come she's so freaked out about the mast?' I ask.

'Because my guess is, she's the sort of woman who loves to have something to complain about.'

'You're not worried about the mast causing health problems, then?'

'I would be if there was any scientific evidence to prove that it does, but as far as I can see, there isn't.'

'But surely Mrs Ravonia must have *some* evidence?'

'The only "evidence" she's got is a lot of hysteria in *The Echo* and Tonya's word that she's been getting migraines lately, which according to Tracey, must be related to the mast because there's no obvious medical explanation for them. And, as she puts it, "My Tonya's no liar."'

'But how d'you know Tonya's not getting headaches?'

'Because the day I moved in I heard her on the balcony laughing down the phone about how she was bunking off school with one of her "mast migraines", and how she'd meet whoever it was down the arcade as usual. If you ask me, the only thing wrong with Tonya Ravonia is she's got two overworked parents who are rarely home to keep an eye on her and who are so soft they believe everything she says.'

I nod like these are the wisest words I've ever heard,

but really I'm thinking: I wish I had two soft parents who believed everything I said.

★ ★ ★

At six o'clock Karen comes to collect me, by order of Mum. When the doorbell goes, Dad whooshes her in and gives her the grand tour before checking the coast's clear of Tonya and walking us down to the car.

'We're picking up Dave on the way,' announces Karen airily, dumping her bag on the front passenger seat. Which translated means, 'You're sitting in the back, Lauren.' As per usual.

Dave lives with his ancient parents, not far from Dad's, behind the Stonebridge council estate. On the drive over Karen seems uneasy. She doesn't switch on the radio, which she usually does when it's just me and her in the car. Out of the corner of my eye I can see her watching me in the rearview mirror.

'Dad seems better now he's got a place of his own, doesn't he?' she says at last, trying to sound casual cool. 'He's seems a bit less . . . lonely, don't you think?'

'Yeah,' I lie, slouching down in my seat.

I wish she would shut up. But of course she blunders on.

'Did you . . . hear anything last night?'

'Like what?'

'Like Mum crying in bed?'

I shake my head and stare fiercely out of the passenger window.

Karen carries on, uncertainly. 'I was thinking . . .

maybe she's regretting all those times she got moody with Dad? Maybe she's sorry about that last big bust-up they had?'

I shudder as the memory of that night comes rushing back: yelling and crying from the kitchen; Mum telling Dad she felt stifled and trapped; Dad shouting if that's how she felt, he'd better go.

Karen again, trying to sound cheery: 'Maybe now he's gone, she realises just how much she misses him. Maybe she wants him back?'

'Maybe,' I mumble, dragging my eyes up to meet hers in the rearview mirror. But I know deep down she doesn't believe that, any more than me.

★ ★ ★

Dave's already out front when we pull up, his hands deep in his jeans' pockets, a fag stuck to his bottom lip.

'Hey, Sexy,' he says, winking at Karen and moving her bag off the front passenger seat.

Karen giggles (talk about horrific), Dave gets into the car, and a fog of cigarette smoke wafts over me. Gro-o-o-ss! Why anyone would want to fill their lungs with something that disgusting beats me. Perhaps it helps take his mind off the fact he's going out with Karen.

Mercifully, the drive home *doesn't* go via Australia; by the time we get in Mum's gone out for a drink with Man-mad Marge, which means there's no one to stop me using the phone in the hallway. Yesss! I wait until 'Sexy' and Dave have gone upstairs to start their snog-athon. Then I call Dex. And Ems. And Nat. And Tash.

And yummy Lee Quick from Year Ten, but I put the phone down the minute he picks up, obviously.

Talking to the gang, we agree a backup plan to stop me getting duffed up by Tonya on Monday:

08.15 hrs: Dex and me catch bus to school, as per usual. (No need for extra backup this end; Tonya's too lazy to come out all the way to my house and Fran hasn't the brains to come on her own. Even if she had, she's no threat by herself.)

08.30 hrs: Ems hovers at school bus stop and keeps her beadies peeled for Tonya and Fran. If sighted, Ems texts me to say stay on bus until next stop.

08.35 hrs: Ems, Dex and me walk from bus stop to main school gate. If Tonya and Fran attack, that's three against two, which is fair. (It'd be fairer if it was four against two, but Tasha says sorry she won't be in on Monday because she's skiving off to meet Gary.)

08.40 hrs: Nat lurks at main school gate and informs us of Tonya's known movements. (Tonya's unlikely to use the side gate because it is a slightly longer walk from her home and she is, as I have said, the laziest person this side of a coma.)

08.41 hrs: If Tonya hasn't arrived, we all leg it to tutor room for registration.

08.41 hrs: If Tonya has arrived – and is possibly

staking out usual route to tutor room – Nat opens window in Science Block, Ems gives me and Dex a leg up, and we scoot to registration from there. (Ems is the tallest, so she's the leg-up person. She's also the broadest and the strongest, but Dex doesn't like it if you point that out.)

Now, you don't need to be Englebert Einstein to see this plan is a work of sheer genius and, come Monday morning, it goes like clockwork: Dex sticks to me like a stalker, Nat hovers like a hovercraft, Ems lurks like a lurker.

Only snag is, Tonya doesn't show up.

'Probably home practising her punch,' puts in Dex helpfully, before dashing off to pin up something about the chess club on the noticeboard.

I don't know if it's the massive relief of not getting head-butted to death or what, but all of a sudden I feel strangely cheerful. Everyone in the grounds is talking about my picture of Tonya. Lee Quick even comes up to me and says, "Nice one," which is gobsmacking because he's never so much as glanced at me before: my heart almost stops with excitement. He says my picture would make a great screen-saver, which later gets me thinking: I must ask Uncle Tim to show me how to change the screen-saver at home. After all, he's the one who got me into this mess in the first place by showing me how to manipulate photos on the computer. Although, to be fair, he didn't know I was then going to put Tonya's head up a horse's bum.

After Lee's strolled off, Ems practically does a jig on the spot.

'He likes you,' she squeals.

Nat grins and nudges me in the ribs. Then, with a serious face, she says, 'You know who I fancy?'

'Who?'

'Bruce Willis.'

'You mean, Bruce Willis the ancient baldy actor, star of *Die Hard 1, 2, 3* and *74*?'

'That's the one!'

Blimey!

By now the three of us are in the corridor on our way to English. As we turn the bend, there's a roar of laughter from the English room. Above the racket I can hear Finbar Cronk going, 'Hil-ARY!' in a high, posh lady's voice.

Dex is still laughing at the joke as we slide into the seats beside him: me first; Nat next to me; Ems on the end, by the door.

Dex leans across his desk and yells above the riot, 'Old Retardo's put up a poster of Hilary in the foyer.'

Nat's freckly face lights up.

'How much do you dare me to draw a Hitler moustache on it?' she says.

Dex goes, 'What are you, mad?'

I say, 'I'll pay you £20 to do it.'

And Ems, straining to hear, shouts, 'What?'

Nat looks me in the eye.

'Have you got £20, Lauren?' she asks archly.

I say, 'No, but I could blackmail it out of Karen.'

And Mr Barnett's huge frame comes through the door just in time to hear Ems yell, 'Who is Loz blackmailing?'

For a moment he glares horribly at me (yes, *me*, even though there's a war going on in the back row!). Then, striding over to his desk, he bellows, 'That's enough!' and the noise level drops dramatically. Dex looks at me as if to say, What was *that* about? And miserably I think: Great! If Hilary's out to impress Mum he's clearly not planning to do it by getting pally with me.

Shooting another harsh look in my direction, Hilary slouches against the front of his desk, then surveys us all wearily. As usual, it's like there's a heavy fog hanging about him.

'Congratulations on your book, Sir,' calls out Tim Smart. The creep.

Hilary smiles uncomfortably and stares at his feet. Then he sucks in a breath and, pushing his bottom off the desk, he booms, 'Can anyone tell me what is an iambic pentameter?'

No one puts their hand up.

He tries again. 'Can any one tell me what is a syllable?'

Dex, Nat and a few other brainy ones stick up their hands.

So, too, does Dottie Dray.

Hilary points to Dottie. 'Yes?'

'Is it a kind of dessert?' she asks seriously, not trying to be funny.

The brainy ones howl; Hilary looks at his watch and sighs, 'Christ', then moving round to the blackboard, he writes: *A syllable is a unit of sound. A syllabub is a pudding.*

The lesson goes downhill from there.

By breaktime my earlier cheerfulness has worn off, and by home-time my brain is so fried from freaking out about Hilary fancying Mum, it hurts. Even the news that he'd had to go home sick after lunch fails to perk me up. Of course, if Mr Noble (my form tutor) weren't so busy flirting with Mrs Martin, he'd have noticed my distress and sent me home to watch *The Simpsons*. But he is, so he doesn't. Instead he reminds me I've got detention for climbing on school property last Thursday, and for not having my shirt tucked in on Tuesday. Or Wednesday.

Weirdly enough, detention turns out to be a bit of a lifesaver because just after last bell, Ems spots Tonya and Fran lurking in the alleyway that Dex and me use as a shortcut to the bus stop. She calls to tell me this marvellous news as I'm catching the bus home.

She begins, 'Loz, sorry to have to tell you this but Tonya and the Stick waited for you in the alleyway for nearly twenty minutes.'

I can practically feel the blood draining from my face. 'Are you sure they were waiting for me?'

'Oh, yeah. Fran had her sleeves rolled up and her hair pulled back out of her eyes, and Tonya was pawing the pavement.'

Oh, Nelly! 'Did they see you?'

'No. I ducked behind a car.'

'Good thinking. Then what?'

'Then I ducked behind another car because the first car drove off.'

38

Good grief!

'Then Tonya had a can of lager and the Stick a couple of fags. Then they both sloped off and I went into town. Which reminds me, guess who I just bumped into coming out of the Babylon Lounge looking rough and *really* smelling of alcohol?'

'The Queen?'

'No.'

'My nan?'

'No. Hilary Barnett!'

'No!'

'Yeah!'

'But he was supposed to be off sick this afternoon!'

'I know!'

My heart sinks like a ship. I think: Dear Lord, isn't it bad enough he hates me? Now that he's after Mum, he's an alcoholic too?

Ems blunders on. 'I was so shocked, I didn't know what to say. I mean, if it'd been Mrs Niblock [our religious studies teacher] you'd think, What's new? But Hilary!'

I force my brain back to the conversation. 'What did he say to you?'

'First he muttered, "Oh, bugger." Then he got a grip and said something about collecting a prescription.'

'Lame!'

'I know! Then he saw I was holding my *A to Z* so he asked me where I was looking for.'

'Where were you looking for?'

'This new shop that sells sheet music.' (For some reason best known to herself, Ems plays the piano.) 'So I said, "I'm looking for Preston Street," and he said, "This is Preston Street." So I said, "Do you know where Maestro Music is?" and he said, "There, under that sign that says Maestro Music.'"

There is a pause.

Then I say matter-of-factly, 'The sign was really huge wasn't it, Ems?'

And she sighs and says, 'Bloody enormous.'

Not long after this news flash, Ems announces she's got to go, and I get to thinking again about Mum dating Hilary and about Tonya slating me, and pretty soon – *Aaargh!* – my stomach's in knots. To make things worse, when I get home I discover:

1. I've forgotten my key.
2. The spare is missing from under the geranium pot by the front door.
3. Mad Mr Peterson from next-door is shouting that he knows I stole his UFO logbook and he can prove it.

I throw back my head and am just about to yell *STREEEESSSS!* at the top of my lungs when who should come galumphing up the front path, dressed in summery black, but Queen Goth herself, Karen.

She says, 'What you doing out here?'

I explain about the missing spare key.

'If it's missing,' she replies, letting herself in with her own key, 'it can only be because *you* didn't put it back the last time you used it.'

'But I did,' I protest angrily.

'Well, let's think it through,' she says sarkily, dropping her college bag on the floor and swivelling her huge bony nose round to face me. 'I never use the spare because I've got the wit to remember my own key. Mum sometimes uses the spare but always puts it back the minute she's opened the door. And you constantly use the spare because you are a clueless moron. So, you tell me, Sherlock, who's the culprit most likely to be? Me, Mum or you of the big bum?'

I stomp down the hallway into the kitchen and slam the door behind me.

I hate Karen.

I really do.

And I'm not just saying that.

In the kitchen, desperately searching for something normal to eat, I think about the missing spare key. The last time I used it was two days ago, on Saturday afternoon, on my way back from Dex's house, and I *know* I put it back under the geranium pot after that. I just know it. So there's no way I'm taking the blame for it being missing. *No way!*

As usual, there is nothing remotely tasty to eat in our Weight Watchers-obsessed house, so I make myself a cheese, mayo and lettuce sandwich – without the cheese, or the mayo – and plod upstairs. And that's when I notice: the door to my bedroom, it's *open*.

Furious and cursing Karen, I storm inside. And freeze.

The place is a total mess. Books have been knocked from the shelves, clothes have been yanked from the drawers, even the mattress has been pulled from the bed.

I don't believe it!

My bedroom has been ransacked!

5

The Stolen Box

For once in her beaky-nosed life, Karen does something useful. The minute she hears me yelling her name, she shoots out of her bedroom, clocks what's happened, arms herself with a broom, and marches round the house to check that the ransacker's not lurking anywhere. He isn't. Then she calls the police and Mum and Dad and Dave – although why we need Dave on the case is a mystery in itself. I mean, what's he going to do, smoke the thief out with one of his fags?

Mum is the first to arrive on the scene, thank goodness. The second she rings the doorbell, I rush to answer it and burst into tears.

'There, there,' she says, wrapping her arms around me like a blanket. 'Don't cry.' She strokes my hair. 'Do you know what's been stolen?'

I wipe my eyes on my sleeve. 'I dunno. I haven't finished looking.'

'Tell you what. Why don't you go upstairs and finish checking? I'll see if anything's missing from the other rooms, and Karen'll make us all a nice cup of tea.'

Just then Karen appears behind me and says, 'Make sure you don't disturb things too much until the police get here.'

And I think: That's all we need, Nancy Drew investigating.

While I'm up in my room, checking, checking, a whisper of panic breezes around my brain: where's the small padlocked box I keep under my bed? Frantically, I claw through the stuff that's been pulled out from under the bed. Then I scrabble about under the frame. But I can't see it anywhere. The whisper is now a shout. Oh, God! Where is it? Where's my box?

Just then the doorbell goes and soon Mum leads two policemen upstairs, followed by Karen, carrying my cup of tea.

'There aren't any signs of a break-in,' I hear Karen babble as they all plod upwards. 'And nothing seems to have been taken. Only Lauren's room has been trashed. And even then, it's just the drawers, desk and under-the-bed stuff that's been searched. That suggests the intruder was looking for something in particular, don't you think?'

Out of politeness neither police officer does say what he thinks, but judging by the look they exchange when they get to my room it's not, What an exceedingly helpful young woman.

Once properly inside my room, the two officers have a look round. While they're taking it all in, Mum and Karen hover in the doorway and I try hard not to freak out about my box.

'What's missing?' asks the shorter officer, who is, it has to be said, insanely *hairy*. (At first I couldn't work out why he was wearing a gorilla suit under his shirt, then I realised he wasn't.)

I tell him about my box, which is marked *Private*.

'What's in this private box?' he asks.

I can feel my cheeks going pink. 'Oh, just letters and photos; stuff like that.'

'What sort of letters and photos?' butts in Nancy Nosey Parker.

Mum leaps in. 'Perhaps the officers would like some tea,' she says pointedly, giving Karen the sort of look that would make a statue jump to it.

Karen jumps to it and disappears downstairs, still clutching my cup of tea.

'Right!' says PC Hairy after Karen has gone. 'Let's try again. What exactly is in this box?'

I stare at my shoes. There's no way I can list everything in my box, I tell myself. *No way*! I mean, suppose he asks why I've got, locked away, Lee Quick's identity bracelet? Or why I'm keeping my first bra, which obviously I'll never fit into again.

I glance up at Mum who gives me a big encouraging smile. I know I've got to say something, so I list all the non-embarrassing stuff that's missing:

'A turquoise stone necklace.' (A present from Joaquin who I met on holiday last year.)

'A letter from Spain.' (Sent to me by Joaquin after I got home.)

45

'A postcard from Spain.' (Joaquin again, asking for his necklace back.)

'Some photos.' (Including a brilliant one of me, Nat, Ems and Tash squashed into a photo booth.)

'A cassette tape of *The Trashers*, which was my Dad's band when he was at school.' (Not sure why I've got this; it's *sooooo* embarrassing.)

'My diary.' (Which if anyone read, I'd die. Seriously.)

When I've finished listing, Hairy Mary frowns at me, thinking. Then he asks a few more questions such as: Do I know anyone who might want to steal my box? (No.) Can anyone confirm that I was at school until 4.30 pm? (D'oh!) Is anything else missing from the house? (Mum says, 'No'.) Then he asks Mum for a private word and the two of them go downstairs followed by PC Hairy's mate, who says he's off to question the neighbours. (Lord help him when he knocks on mad Mr Peterson's door is all I can say.)

The minute the three of them have gone, I creep out onto the landing, ready to tiptoe downstairs to earwig what's happening. But no sooner have I sneaked over to the top stair than the doorbell goes and Dad is whooshed straight through into the lounge by Mum. I wait until I hear the lounge door shut firmly behind them then carry on tiptoeing. I am just about to press my ear up against the keyhole when the door opens sharply and Dad's head pops round.

'Bloody hell, Loz!' he exclaims as I leap up like a Pop-Tart in a toaster. 'What are you doing?' I pretend to be examining the doorframe. 'Here,' he continues, pressing forty quid into my hand, 'go down to the China Garden and pick up a special set dinner for four. And try not to eavesdrop any more conversations while you're about it.'

The whole way down to the takeaway and back I panic about my box and who might've stolen it, but nothing I come up with makes sense. I mean, the only person who'd want the Joaquin stuff is Joaquin and he's not exactly going to come over from Spain to get it. Then there's my diary, which could be used to blackmail me, I know, but the only people I've told about it are Mum, Dad, Nan Cracknell, Nana Taylor, Granddad, Dex, Nat, Tasha, Ems, Kerry and Eleanor – and none of them would nick it. As for Lee Quick's identity bracelet – well, the only person who saw me take that was Tasha and she would never split on me. Would she?

Thinking about Lee's bracelet, I feel a terrible rush of guilt. I hadn't meant to keep it. Really I hadn't. I'd only meant to borrow it before first bell on Friday for this stupid love spell Ems had gone on about. But when I went to casually drop it back with his stuff by the school railings, he and his mates had finished playing football and his stuff had gone.

Remembering my bracelet shame on top of everything else makes me feel wobbly. By the time I get back home I'm so bunched up inside with worry I hardly notice Karen grabbing the takeaway bags from my hands and putting the warm aluminium cartons on the table.

'Dinner!' she yells in her headmistress voice. And before you can say egg fried rice, we're all sitting down to eat – PC Hairy Mary and his mate long gone.

Now, at first I don't notice anything; I'm too busy chewing and panicking and half-listening to Nancy Drew blundering on about how the thief must be someone we know because they used the spare key, and how we'll need to get a locksmith out because we don't want every psycho and drug addict in town running around with a copy of our front door key. But after a while, I'm aware of something unnerving: Mum and Dad keep looking at me out of the corner of their eyes then glancing back at each other. It's like they've got me under secret surveillance . . . and I haven't the faintest foggiest why.

Later that evening, after Dad has gone and my room has been tidied (sort of), I shove my head under my duvet and call Dex. I have to ring from under my duvet because I'm only supposed to use my mobile for emergencies and texting, and if Mum hears me chatting at this hour, she'll go into orbit and stop topping up my phone.

He picks up, *at last*. 'Yo.'

'It's me.'

'Lozzie?'

'Yes.'

'I can hardly hear you.'

'That's because I'm whispering under the duvet.'

'Of course. I knew there'd be a perfectly sane explanation.'

'Dex, let me ask you something. Do your parents ever

look at you like they know you're up to something when you're not?'

'All the time. Why, what have you done?'

'Nothing. But I have been burgled.'

'*No!*'

And I give him a complete rundown of everything that's happened and everything that's missing – everything except my Lee Quick stuff, that is; Dex can be a bit funny about him.

'Well, it's obvious, isn't it?' he says when I'm finished. 'The thief is Tonya!'

'*Tonya!* Oh, c'mon Dex, be sensible! Tonya's a bruiser not a burglar.'

''Ow do you know, my friend? Just becoz . . .'

I interrupt, 'Dex, is that a Hercule Poirot accent you're doing?'

Silence.

'As I was saying, Lauren . . .'

He was doing a Hercule Poiret accent, you know.

'Tonya is the thief. She has the motive. And the opportunity. She was off sick today, remember?'

'Yeah, but what about the missing spare key?'

'Ah, yes! The geranium pot by the front door! What amateur burglar could crack that kind of brilliant security? Face it, Loz, *everyone* knows where your spare key is kept: your neighbours, passers-by, anyone who's ever seen you or your mum letting yourselves in . . .'

'All right, all right. But Tonya's never come round here with me or Mum. She never even comes out this far. Why would she?'

'Dunno. All I know is, she found the key, she let herself in, and she nicked your box, for revenge. Case closed.'

After Hercule gets off the phone, I have a think about what he's said. OK, so Tonya had the motive and the opportunity. But is burglary really her style? And if it is, wouldn't the whole house have been trashed? And if it had been wrecked, wouldn't way more stuff have been taken, such as my DVDs and Mum's lager for starters?

6
Freak-outs

Next morning (Tuesday) I wake up with a major headache. I stumble to the bathroom for a couple of paracetamols and bump into Mum.

'Morning, love,' she says, looking like she hasn't slept much, either. 'I was wondering, how would you like to take today off school?'

I blink at her. 'Huh?'

'You've been looking tired lately and after yesterday I thought a day off school might do you good.'

Now, this is beyond weird! I mean, never once in all the centuries I've been going to school has Mum ever let me skive off. Even when I had food poisoning and was on my dying deathbed, she still wanted proof I wasn't faking.

I examine her face close-up. There can be only one rational explanation for this, I tell myself. And that is – her mind has been taken over by Martians.

In which case, I'm making the most of it.

'That'd be great, Mum.'

'Good. I'll ring Christelle and get her to cover for

me. Then once the locksmith's been, we can do a bit of girly shopping together in town.'

Now my jaw *really* hits the floor. Mum *never* takes time off work. Ever. Even when she sprained her ankle leaping about to *Tainted Love* with Man-mad Marge in the kitchen (don't ask), she still hobbled into work the next day.

'OK,' I say, totally confused. 'That'd be cool.'

And it is.

Sort of.

We check out the shops, try on the wigs in Debenhams, and have lunch in Caffè Nero. Mum even buys me this fab bag for school with see-through plastic slots on one side, for putting your favourite photos in. But even though we're having fun, shopping, shopping, shopping, Mum seems nervy, distracted, worried. It's as if she's working herself up to say something huge.

And when we get home, out it comes.

Like an unstoppable flood.

'I know you're angry at me and your dad for breaking up,' she splurts out suddenly, at the sink, doing the dishes.

'No, Mum. I'm not.'

'Well, you're angry just at me then because you think it's all my fault Dad moved out.'

'No, Mum, I'm . . .'

'No, no, that's fine; it's perfectly understandable. No one's blaming you. We all get angry when we feel powerless in a situation we want to control, and in those circumstances it's natural to want to lash out and make someone pay . . .'

Mum is whisking the washing-up brush round Nana's antique china bowl at jet propellor speed.

'When I feel powerless and frustrated there's a part of me that wants to blow my top, lash out, smash things up . . .'

Blimey! If Mum's not careful the brush will lift-off like a helicopter and have her eye out.

'So I can understand if that's what you felt like doing, of course I can . . .'

I don't believe it! Mum's actually scrubbed the gold pattern off Nana's bowl.

'I know, I know, it's not just the separation . . .'

I inspect the pattern-less bowl as I dry it.

'I'm always working and . . .'

Nana is going to go ballistic when she sees what's happened to her heirloom.

'You're under a lot of pressure at school and I haven't been here enough to support you, I know, I know, and I take full responsibility for that . . .'

Hold on! What does she mean 'pressure at school'? Dad better not've told her about Tonya.

'But you must understand, love, bottling things up until you blow up into a rage and trash your stuff isn't the answer . . .'

WHAT?!

'Not in the long-term. You need to *tell* someone if you're feeling angry . . .'

She's not suggesting I trashed my room *myself*, is she?

'I'm not saying it has to be me. If you can't talk to me, talk to Dad. I won't be offended. And I won't be cross.

Neither will the police. Honestly. Even if there were drugs in your box . . .'

Drugs? I'm on drugs?

'And things have got out of hand and you're in with a bad crowd and someone was after your gear or stash, or whatever it's called . . .'

Stash? Now I'm a dealer with a stash!

'You can't cope with this by yourself. It's far too much. All I ask is just please, *please* talk to us and tell us . . .'

Oh, I'll talk to you all right, I fume. And flinging down my tea towel, I yell, 'MUM' so loudly, she screams. Then I fix her with a steely stare and in a strict, harsh voice say, 'Listen up, Mother. I did not trash my room; there were no drugs in my box; I am not on drugs; I am not supplying drugs; and I'm not pregnant, glue sniffing or shoplifting, either! OK?'

For a second she stares at me, dumbstruck. Then her whole body sags with relief.

'Oh, thank you, Jesus, Mary and Joseph,' she gushes. 'Thank you, thank you.'

And I storm upstairs, hurl myself onto my bed and scream into my pillow.

Inside my head I rave like a loony. What *is* it with mothers? What? *What?* What is their problem? Is there some great parent manual out there they all read that says, Not sure what's going on? Here's the answer: jump to the wrong conclusion and GO MENTAL. I mean, how *could* she accuse me of taking drugs? And how *dare* she say I hang out with a bad crowd? If anyone is hanging out with a bad crowd, it's *her*! Man-mad Marge is hardly Little Miss Perfect! I've seen her drink Bacardi Breezers for breakfast!

I roll onto my back and glare murderously at the ceiling. Actually, it's a major miracle I'm not on drugs when you come to think about it. First the break-up. Then the endless shuttling back and forth between Mum and Dad like a toy they've got to share. Then Tonya. Then 'Hilary'. Next the theft of my diary and crush stuff. Now this. Bloody Nora! How much more can one girl take?

Just then my mobile rings.

It's Dex.

With a message from Tonya.

7

Cringe and Chips

'Yo!' says Dex when I pick up. 'How come you weren't at school today?'

'I was skiving.'

There is a pause while he relays this info to Ems, whose mobile, I guess, he's using. Then he says, 'Does your mum know?'

'She suggested it.'

'*No!* How come?'

I sigh. 'It's a *looo*ng story.'

'Oh! OK. Erm . . . I've got a message for you. From Tonya.'

There is a heart-stopping silence. 'OK.'

'Well, the good news is you don't have to watch your back on the way to school any more.'

'*Really? Tonya's forgiven me then?*'

'Oh, yeah. She's forgiven you all right. She's so full of forgiveness she's threatening now to ram your head down the toilet and flush it 'til you drown.'

I let out a squeak.

'You OK?'

In the background I can hear Ems asking, 'Is she OK?'

I try to speak but all that comes out is 'Nghhh!' I try again. 'Dex?'

'Yeah?'

'What do you think it'd take to stop Tonya from drowning me?'

'Mass destruction of the Earth by a meteorite?'

I groan; he says, 'Sorry' then carries on. 'Look, Ems is off to her music lesson and I'm about to get the bus home, then I've got to pick up Ed from karate and drop him off at The Diner. *Soooo*, whaddya say we meet up there at, er, quarter to five?'

The Diner is this great café owned by Dex's parents on the High Street, just a couple of doors along from the salon. When I tell Mum where I'm heading she slaps on her let's-pretend-nothing's-happened smile and says, 'Great! I was thinking of going into the salon. We could walk down together.'

I shoot her a look as if to say, *Yeah, right! Mrs Big Drugs Expert.* And clutching my new bag, I march off on my own.

Stomping along the High Street, just before crossing over for The Diner, I make the fatal mistake of looking in Harper's Bookshop's window. Unbelievably, there's now a *display* of Hilary's stupid book to go with his stupid poster. On the front cover, underneath the words *Haunts of the Black-eyed Girl*, there's a photograph of a blank piece of paper in a typewriter. Now, what's that got to do with being haunted or having black eyes? I mean, how crap a cover is that?

For once The Diner is really quiet. I nip straight into the booth nearest the door, next to the window, and after a bit, Mrs F (Dex's mum) comes beetling over, looking thin and worn-out.

'Hello Lauren, luvvie,' she says. 'You not with Dex?'

I explain about having the day off school because of the break-in, and she says how sorry she was when she heard, and that she'll give Mum a call later. Then she asks if I'd like anything to eat or drink – I say, 'A cup of hot chocolate, please'– and soon she's back with a huge mug of steaming chocolate in one hand and a chocolate muffin in the other. The hot chocolate has mini marsh-mallows on top and everything.

I really, really like Dex's parents' café, and not just because of the free food and drink. It's like it's stuck in a time warp. The walls are crammed with black-framed posters of old films. In one corner is an enormous juke-box that Mr F bought without consulting Mrs F. And at right angles to the walls and to the street-facing win-dow are these booths that have wine-coloured padded benches with really high backs. There's something dead cosy about sitting in these booths, probably because the seat backs hide you from the people sitting at the tables either side. Once I had this dream that I was curled up in the booth by the jukebox and Lee Quick came in. He sidled up to me and without saying a word, slowly, slowly moved his lips towards mine. I closed my eyes and was just about to melt into *the* most *DIVINE* kiss when, out of nowhere, my nan popped up and yelled, 'Good God, I've gone bald!' Next thing I know, wigs are flying overhead and I'm chasing a runaway pig across Scotland.

Thinking about Nan Cracknell and Lee Quick in the same dream must've made me go green or something because when Christelle comes into the café two seconds later, the first thing she says to me is, 'Oh, la la! You look like you see a ghost.'

I smile and go, 'It's OK. I'm fine.'

And she plonks her bag on my table.

As usual, she's looking really cool. Her hair's dead short and bleached blonde, and her work shirt, with *A Cut Above* printed on the back, is tied in a knot at her tiny waist.

'I am sorry to hear of your burglary,' she says, rooting around in her bag for her purse. 'I get a cappuccino, yes, and I come back for ze quick chat?'

While she's up at the counter ordering a takeaway coffee, I spy an advert for a flat poking out from her bag. I pull it out and take a closer look. Wow! Nice doesn't even begin to describe this place. It looks so modern and stylish.

'You buying a flat, Christelle?' I ask when she returns with her polystyrene cup.

She goes a bit pink. 'I 'ope so,' she says, smiling nervously. She perches on the edge of the seat opposite me and takes back the advert. 'I am soon to get some money zat should've gone to Mercedes.'

Christelle lives up behind the High Street's post office, in a tiny rented flat Mum says is dark and depressing.

I sigh heavily. 'I wish I was about to get some money.

That way I could hire a hitman to assassinate Tonya.'

'Who is zis Tonya?'

'The devil disguised as a blancmange.'

Christelle smiles and buries the advert deep in her bag, and I carry on.

'Won't you be sad leaving your little flat after so long?' I ask.

No sooner are the words out of my mouth than I regret it. But too late. Christelle's face crumples.

'For me, eet is too lonely living zere wizout Mercedes.' She stares out of the window. 'I thought eet would be more easy if I pack up all 'er belongings from around ze flat and shut zem away in a room, *mais non*. Still the flat has so much memories.'

For one dreadful moment I think Christelle is going to cry, but just in time she gives herself a little shake, gets to her feet and scoops up her coffee and bag.

'I 'ave to return to ze salon now,' she says briskly. 'I need to use ze computer before my client at five o'clock. See you soon, *oui*?'

And before I can say sorry, she's gone.

Two miserable bites of chocolate muffin later, Dex strolls into the café followed by Ed. I give a little wave, Dex flops down opposite me, and Ed comes up really close and fixes me with his fish eye stare.

'Al Capone once killed a man for borrowing his car,' he says flatly.

I look at Dex like, *What the . . . ?* and Mrs F darts over, puts her hands on Ed's shoulders and gently turns him round to face the counter.

'Pop out back, love, and get Dad to make you some cheese on toast,' she says.

Reluctantly, the little freak does as he's told; Mrs F turns to Dex.

'Now, my lovely . . .' She is looking doubtfully at the slicked back style he's trying with his hair. 'I expect you'll be wanting something too.'

Dex grins and orders egg and chips and a cup of tea; I say I'm fine with my chocolate muffin; and soon, we're chomping and slurping and nattering away.

'What am I gonna do about Tonya and my box?' I moan. 'This whole death-by-drowning revenge thing is doing my head in!'

Dex swallows a fistful of chips. 'Just keep well clear of her until the summer holidays start. You should be OK after that.'

'Hmm. And what do you suggest I do toilet-wise in the meantime, seeing as how her life ambition is to corner me in the bogs and flush my head down the loo?'

Dex dips a chip into his egg. 'Go before you get to school and hold the rest in till you get home?'

I snort and nick one of his chips; he shouts, 'Oi!' I change the subject.

'So what did I miss today?'

Dex hoovers up his last bit of egg. 'Er . . . Nat got given three lunchtime detentions by Old Retardo for drawing a Hitler moustache on Hilary's poster in the foyer . . .'

'How did he know it was Nat?'

'The marker pen she'd used fell out of her sleeve while he was questioning her.'

'Unlucky.'

'And Hilary burst a blood vessel at Sam Pushpanathan.'

'How come?'

'Oh, the usual. He asked if anyone could give him an example of a simile and Akin put his hand up and said, "My uncle drinks like a fish," and Sam chipped in, "He's not the only one, I hear," and we all cracked up.'

Dex takes a sip of his tea.

'By the way,' he continues, leaning back from the table, 'what was it you were gonna tell me on Saturday when you rang from the salon party?'

For a moment my mind goes totally blank. Then I can almost feel the bulb inside my brain light up. Hilary and Mum. *Hilary and Mum!* What with Tonya and Operation Backup and the burglary and daydreaming about Lee, I hadn't got round to telling Dex about Hilary fancying Mum! Instantly, I fill him in on everything: on Man-mad Marge's bombshell; on Mum describing the Fartman as intelligent and interesting; on my horror at the possibility of her dating the moodiest, sarkiest man alive.

All the time I'm gabbing away Dex just stares at me. Then at last, he bursts out, 'This is major! This is huge!'

'*Tell me about it!*' I explode, and for a moment we sit goggling at each other like doughnuts.

Dex is the first to break eye contact. He takes off his glasses and wipes them slowly with the end of his shirt. Then: 'You know something?' he says, putting his specs back on. 'I don't think that invite you posted through Hilary's door was an invitation to the salon party.'

'How do you mean?'

'The invites were for your mum's regular customers only, right? But Hilary can't be a regular customer. He's bald.'

It takes a couple of beats for this to sink in. Then I have a scary thought.

'Oh, Nelly! You don't suppose the invite was something, you know, *personal* from Mum?'

'Like what?'

'Like a card asking him on a date?'

Dex crinkles his forehead. 'Wouldn't she just text him or email him if she wanted to ask him out?'

'Dunno. But I do know Lucy often writes her boyfriend lovey-dovey cards and puts them in the salon's out-tray for Christelle to take to the post office on her way home, so maybe Mum just copied her and . . .'

But Dex is no longer listening. He's staring up past my head, his face stone still. I swivel my own head to follow his gaze. And there, standing behind me, is Hilary Barnett.

In the flesh.

His face, absolutely *furious!*

8

Investigation: Pet Shop

'Well, *that* was shameful!' says Dex after Hilary has left.

My heart drops down from my throat and my head crashes into my hands.

'*Ohnooooooooo!*' I wail. 'He must've been sitting behind me the whole time I've been here. What did I say? What did I say?' Quickly I rewind my brain back to my chat with Christelle then fast forward onto my conversation with Dex. 'Oh. My. God. I called him moody and sarky.'

'And Fartman. You called him Fartman, too.'

I thunk my head on the top of the table and groan. And as I'm thunking and groaning, the door to the café bangs open and I hear Flo come shuffling in. Flo is our neighbourhood bag lady. She's tiny and crinkly and very confused, and she always wears an enormous green coat, a brown woolly hat and a pair of Barbie pink slippers. There are many weird things about Flo – the coat, the hat and the slippers for starters. But the weirdest thing of all is she never looks depressed, which you'd think she would, seeing as how she once was a famous artist's model, and now she lives out of plastic bags. In fact, she's always got this trace of a smile on her lips. Dave reckons she must smoke some serious stuff to look that chilled. But I think it's because in her mind, she's living in California with some ancient man she fancies, probably Mick Jagger of The Rolling Stones or maybe Bruce Springsteen.

'Yo, Flo,' chirps Dex as her plastic bags rustle past our booth.

I drag my head up off the table and am just about to say hello as well when I catch sight of something familiar safety-pinned to the back of her hat. I look again, and sure enough, there it is: my stolen turquoise stone necklace!

I grab Dex's arm, practically sending his teacup flying.

'Look!' I hiss. 'Look! Flo's got my necklace safety-pinned to her hat.'

And leaping up, I dash down to her corner booth and hover awkwardly while she sits herself down.

'Hello, Flo,' I say when she's settled herself, *at last*.

She gives me her faraway smile. 'I've still got the figure of a young woman, you know.'

I press my lips together. This is going to be like talking to my nan after she's been at the whisky. I carry on, 'Flo, I was wondering, the necklace on your hat, where did you get it from?'

'It was a gift. From an admirer.'

Right. 'And do you know who this admirer is?'

'Of course, I do. The Duke of York.'

The Duke of York? Oh, Nelly! I suck in a breath.

'And do you know where the Duke of York got your necklace from?'

But Flo doesn't answer. Her eyes are riveted to something imaginary on the ceiling. I ask her again if she knows where my necklace came from. And again. But it's no use. She's miles away – off, off, off in sunny California, with Mick and Bruce and probably this Duke bloke, too.

I am just deciding what to do next when Mrs F comes scurrying up.

'Here you go, Flo, luvvie,' she says kindly, placing a cup of tea and a toasted cheese sandwich on the tabletop. 'Don't let it get cold.'

Mrs F always gives Flo a free cup of tea and something warm to eat when she comes into the café. Dex once asked his mum why she did this, and she said, 'There, but for the grace of God, go I,' which, as Dex pointed out, is yet more proof that parents are completely incapable of giving a simple answer to anything unless, of course, the question is, Can I get my bellybutton pierced? In which case the answer is always a definite, No.

Anyhow – back to The Diner.

I turn to Mrs F and say hopefully, 'You don't know where Flo got that necklace on her hat from, do you?'

Mrs F glances over at Flo who is now mesmerised by something imaginary on the table.

'From a bin, I expect. That's where she collects most of her belongings from. I've seen her going through those new bins along Eastern Road in town quite a few times now, and occasionally the one outside the Duke of York's cinema, too.'

At the mention of the Duke of York's my heart does a back flip. Quickly, I say, 'Oh. Right. Er . . . thanks.' And I shoot back to Dex.

'C'mon!' I say, grabbing my bag. 'We're going.'

'Now?'

'Yeah.'

'Where to?'

'To town.'

'How come?'

'To check out the bin by the Duke of York's.'

'Any particular reason?'

'Yep. I think that's where my box might be.'

Now you'd think the sight of two teenagers rummaging through a rubbish bin outside a cinema would send some passer-by into a tutting fit. But even though the street is busy, no one bats an eyelash. Which is fine with me.

I suck in a breath, lower my hands into the half-filled bin and pull out a couple of polystyrene chip trays, a T-shirt splattered with ketchup and a bashed up burger box. Dex makes the face of someone who's just seen a particularly horrific mound of dog poo and picks up a crisp packet using the tips of two fingers.

'That better not be pee I can smell,' he says, his nose wrinkled.

Ignoring him, I pick out a large paper bag of empty

lager cans and a soggy newspaper splattered with something I daren't even try to identify. Dex, ever helpful, picks up another crisp packet and so we go on until, at last, there it is: my box, standing on its side, lid slightly open, sticking out of a white plastic carrier bag. With heart thumping, I lift it out of the plastic bag and place it on the pavement right way up. Then I flip open the lid – and let out a whoosh of relief. Inside is my diary. *Hallelujah!* I'm so relieved, I could cry.

'Anything missing?' asks Dex, crouching down beside me.

I riffle through the box.

'Only Dad's *Thrashers* cassette and a bracelet,' I reply, thinking: Oh, Nelly! Was Flo wearing Lee's identity bracelet, too?

Dex says, 'Maybe they fell out into the plastic bag.'

I lift the bag out of the bin and take a look. There's no sign of Lee's bracelet, only Dad's cassette tape, all cracked and broken like someone's used it as a trampoline.

'Anything else in the bag?' asks Dex, as I shove Dad's busted cassette into my box.

I put my hand inside again and pull out a small bit of paper.

'Just a till receipt,' I reply, starting to read, 'from Pam-Purred Pets on Eastern Road, dated June 9, for a book called *Tortoise Care . . .*'

My voice trails off as Dex's eyes switch to full beam.

'Aw, c'mon,' I cry, at last. 'Just because Tonya's got a tortoise doesn't mean the receipt is hers. Or that she nicked my box. In fact, the receipt doesn't even mean the thief bought the book. She or *he* could've been given the bag in a charity shop or something with the receipt already inside.'

Dex's eyes are shining like headlights in a tunnel. 'Yeah but still, it'd be worth going to PamPurred Pets after school tomorrow to see if the sales assistant remembers who bought the book. Let's face it, there can't be many people fitting Tonya's description.'

He has a point.

'And I know she goes to the Duke of York's coz Ali Pataudi's dad works there and he told Ali he had to throw her out twice for kicking the drinks' vending machine.'

I think about this for a second. Then: 'Hold on! If Tonya nicked my box and stuff, how come she just dumped it all here? It doesn't make sense. My diary contains some pretty explosive material, you know, that she could easily've used against me.'

Dex tips back his head and howls with laughter. 'I don't call scrawling, "I hate Karen" over and over explosive.'

'There's more in it than that,' I huff. 'There's stuff about . . .' The bulb goes on. 'Hey, wait a minute! How come you know what's in my diary?'

Dex stops laughing and quickly starts putting the rubbish back in the bin.

I don't believe it!

'My diary is private, you know!'

Dex keeps on with his stupid head-down, rubbish-putting-back routine.

'So what else did you read?'

'Nothing! Nothing else, I promise.'

'Liar!'

'Honestly. I couldn't read your handwriting. You know, you really should do something about that. My aunt Theresa used to have mad-woman handwriting like yours, then she went on a course and now her writing is really neat.'

Handwriting course? First, traitor-boy sticks his nose into my diary. Now he's telling me I should make it more readable! I shoot him my worst look – the one reserved for murderers, rapists and Karen – and storm off to the bus stop, my box pressed to my chest.

'Aw, c'mon, Loz,' he bleats, half-walking, half-running after me like someone with a wonky hip – which he soon will have if he comes anywhere near me. 'I'm sorry. I didn't mean to read it, honest. And I didn't read anything juicy.'

I spin round to face him.

'Oh, by the way,' I say casually, ignoring the fact that he's only just managed to stop himself from slamming into me. 'You know you were asking who should play you in the film of your life? Well, I was thinking, how about Slitheen from *Doctor Who*? You know, that disgusting green monster that goes around disguised as a human being.'

Dex and I do not speak on the bus journey home. Possibly because he's sitting up front near the driver and I'm on the bus behind.

School the next day (Wednesday) is a total nightmare and that's not including the double chemistry. On the bus journey in, traitor-boy jabbers away about the burglary even though it's obvious I'm not officially speaking to him. And when we get to school, Tonya and Fran are already lurking inside, which means Ems has to give me and Dex a leg up through the Science Block window so that we can scurry to our tutor room safely.

All through break, Bully Blancmange watches me like a fat, piggy-eyed lion waiting for a poor injured gazelle to get separated from the herd. After lunch, she hovers threateningly outside the girls' loos. No wonder when Mrs Hutchin, our history teacher, tells us, 'Ordinary citizens had to be ever vigilant during the Second World War,' I feel like shouting, 'What's new?' Only once during the whole day do I have a laugh – when, in class, Jack Mulrenan says, 'General erection' instead of 'General election'. And even then I have to be careful in case I laugh so hard I end up rushing to the loos without backup. Honestly, if it hadn't been for Tasha saying how great my new bag is and admiring the photos I'd put in the slots, there'd have been no point in living.

Things aren't any less pants after school, either. Dex still hasn't twigged that I haven't forgiven him properly, and is all chatty chat chat about Investigation Pet Shop Receipt.

'I reckon we're gonna crack the case,' he burbles as we slip out of the side gate, shielded by an unsuspecting gang of Year Eleven boys. I mumble if he doesn't stop wittering on, it'll be more than the case that gets cracked, but he just says, 'Are you on your period?' which puts me in an even worse mood.

Outside the side gate, Lee Quick is talking to a pretty red-haired girl from St Bernadettes who's giving him flirty looks. I stride past supercool, pretending I'm not bothered, but deep inside I bloody hate that girl. I really do.

For reasons best known to himself, Dex decides to *power walk* to the pet shop, which means I practically have to run to keep up with him. As we hurtle along at one hundred kilometres an hour, I remember to ring Mum to let her know I'll be late home, only to discover my phone's run out of battery. I let out a groan. Excellent. Now when I get in, I'm going to be treated to that marvellous lecture entitled, What's-The-Point-In-Having-A-Mobile-Phone-If-It's-Never-Switched-On/Recharged/Remembered?

★ ★ ★

The pet shop is right down the far end of Eastern Road, next to a scary looking tattoo parlour. By the time we reach it Dex is so fired up, it's a wonder he doesn't burst into flames. I grab his sleeve just as he's reaching for the door handle.

'Hold on, Hercule,' I pant. 'Before you go charging in, we need to get our story straight.'

He stops. Reluctantly.

I carry on, 'We want to know whether the receipt we

found with my box belongs to Tonya, yeah? So, what we'll say is this: we're friends of hers and we want to get her a book on tortoises for her birthday, but we think she may've bought it for herself last Friday, so can the shopkeeper tell us whether he remembers serving her. OK?'

Dex nods impatiently then pushes open the door.

'Excuse me,' he cries, bounding up to the counter. 'Did you see a friend of ours in here last Friday with shoulder-length blonde hair, tiny brown eyes, really white skin and a tragically massive body?'

The shopkeeper, who is about one hundred and four, eyes Dex up and down.

'You what?'

'She really loves tortoises,' I chip in brightly, 'and we want to buy her a book called *Tortoise Care,* but we just want to check she didn't come in on Friday the ninth of June, and buy it for herself.'

The shopkeeper peers down at me through his glasses, which are as thick as the bottom of a bottle of Coke. I smile up at him sweetly.

'No, I haven't sold anything to anyone looking like that,' he says. 'In fact . . .' He opens a huge exercise book on the counter and runs a knobbly finger down a hand-written list. 'We've only shifted two copies of that book in the last month. One, my wife sold, and the other was to a fella in a Whitcombe Wanderers' shirt. I remember him particularly because you don't see many Whit-combe fans down here on the south coast, do you?'

At the words 'Whitcombe Wanderers', my heart goes

as cold as a frog.

'I'll tell you who bought the other copy,' pipes up a thin voice from out the back. We turn to look as a woman with a face as brown and wrinkled as a walnut appears in the doorway behind the counter. 'It was that writer chappie who's in all the bookshop windows. He doesn't come in here often but I recognised him immediately.'

At the mention of Mr B, Dex practically keels over in amazement but weirdly, I feel scarily calm and still. Slowly, I lift my bag up onto the counter and turn the slotted side to face the shopkeeper.

'Did the Whitcombe fan look like him?' I ask in a small voice, pointing to a photo of Dad wearing a T-shirt that says, World's Greatest Dad.

The shopkeeper lowers his Coke bottle eyes to look at the photo.

'Yes, that's him,' he says, clearly surprised. 'Is he your father?'

I nod dumbly.

'He's certainly mad keen on tortoises, isn't he? He's not long asked me to recommend a breeder who'll supply him with a job lot.'

9

A Date with Doom

Outside the pet shop, I stand in a daze. My brain feels like porridge; my legs like they're dead.

'So, possibly not Tonya then?' says Dex quietly, at last.

'Possibly not.'

'Well, maybe you were right,' he says pretending to be cheery. 'Maybe the receipt doesn't mean anything. Maybe your dad or Hilary left the receipt in the bag and the thief got given the bag in a charity shop, like you said, and then dumped your box in it.'

'Maybe,' I reply miserably.

But then again, maybe not.

Like a zombie in a trance, I walk back up Eastern Road. As I sleepwalk along, Dex by my side, two thoughts struggle through the fog in my head: why would Dad or Hilary want to steal my box? And what is Dad doing buying tortoises by the busload?

Dex is clearly on the same wavelength. 'Why would your dad or Hilary want to steal your box?'

I shrug my shoulders.

'Since when has your dad been into tortoises?'

Another shrug.

'Why would Hilary want a book on them?'

'Dunno.' Then: 'Oh, wait! Actually I do know. He's got a tortoise. I saw it in his front garden when I delivered his salon invite.'

At this Dex's eyebrows practically shoot up into space.

'*Really?* A grown man with a pet tortoise? How sad is that!'

Just then he remembers that my dad also has a pet tortoise – or ten – and his face goes as red as a radish.

Pretending not to notice, I keep walking, head down, trying to force my porridge-of-a-brain to think. But all I come up with is this: the only thing worth nicking from my box was my diary, but Hilary wouldn't be interested in that – why would he? As for Dad, well, it's insane. Why would he want to read my most secret, private thoughts?

Over and over, my brain plods down these same dead-ends. Then: 'You know what?' I announce suddenly, like I've just invented elastic or something. 'We've got two suspects in the frame, yeah? One we can't interrogate, for obvious reasons, but the other, we can. The minute I get home I'm gonna call Dad!'

'Excellent idea,' says Dex encouragingly, then his face cracks into a grin.

'What? What's so funny?' I demand.

'*In the frame?* What are you now, Detective Inspector Cracknell?'

And we both laugh.

When I get home Mum's on the phone in the hallway, a dreamy smile on her lips. The second she sees me the smile vanishes, her lips pinch tight and she jabs a finger at her watch. I say, 'Sorry' and scoot into the kitchen fast. The mobile phone lecture is not a short one and I need to build up my strength. As I'm closing the door behind me I hear Mum say softly into the receiver, 'Yes, tomorrow at six.' Then in a silky whisper she adds, 'I'm looking forward to it.'

Straightaway my radar switches to danger alert, but before I can even begin to pray, Please God, no! Not a date! Karen looks up from her bowl of cereal on the table.

'What happened this time?' she smirks. 'Forget how to press the *on* button on your phone?'

I'm in the middle of chanting, 'Die! Die! Die!' when Mum comes barrelling through the kitchen door.

'And where have you been?' she fumes.

'Hanging out with Dex.'

'Why didn't you ring to say you'd be late?'

'I couldn't. My battery needs recharging.'

'Good God, Lozzie!' she explodes. 'How many more times?' And so the lecture begins: What's the point in me having a mobile phone if I never remember to recharge it? Having a mobile phone is a costly luxury and I need to remember that. It's about time I stopped being so absent-minded and learnt to concentrate on the task in hand. It's not that I don't have a good brain, it's just that I never use it. Etcetera, etcetera, etcetera.

I wait for Mum to stop fizzing – finally – then drag my eyes up from the floor.

'Can I use the phone to ring Dad?' I ask.

Queen Cow butts in.

'No point,' she says, getting up from the table to put her bowl in the sink. 'I've just tried him and his phone's not on.' Then, with her back to Mum, she gives me a sickly sweet smile and says innocently, 'Perhaps he forgot to recharge the battery.'

Mum jumps in. 'Dad's up in Whitcombe for the cricket. He's staying with Uncle Nigel and you know the mobile reception up there's not good. You can ring him when he's back on Friday.'

Friday? What! How long a wait is *that*?

Wednesday is Mum's evening at Weight Watchers and Karen's at Self Defence – although why with a nose like hers she needs to learn how to defend herself beats me. I wait for the two of them to push off before beginning my all-important Wednesday night ritual:

1. Stick on music. (Loud.)
2. Check out what's new in Karen and Mum's rooms. (Karen's got a bottle of *Relaxing Bath Balm* by Clarins hidden in her underwear drawer, and Mum's bought a really low-cut top, which I pray to Heaven is not for Hilary's benefit.)
3. Whizz through homework. (Tonight, double French, which doesn't have to be in until Friday.)
4. Run bath and pour in bubbly stuff. (This evening I'm using *Relaxing Bath Balm* by Clarins.)

So there I am in the bathroom, bubble bath in hand, wondering whether I should top up the bottle with shampoo or water, when what happens? The phone rings. And who should it be on the other end of the line? *Lee Quick!*

He says, 'How come your mobile's not on?'

I'm so stunned he's rung, all I can stutter is, 'Er . . . battery.'

There is a pause while this world-shattering bit of information sinks in. Then he says, 'Do you want to come round mine next Monday after school?' And before my brain can hook up with my mouth, I gush, 'Yeah. Great. Yeah.'

After that, the conversation really starts to buzz. He says, 'Result!' I say, 'Yeah!' He says, 'Bye.' I say, 'Bye.' Then I put the receiver down and stare at the top of the telephone table, trying to stop my stomach from going flip flop, flip flop. And as I stare, flip flop, stare, flip flop, I notice the notepad beside the phone. On it in Mum's handwriting are the words:

Babylon Lounge
Thursday, 6 pm

And surrounding this is a load of love heart doodles.

Instantly all thoughts of Lee vanish from my head and my brain starts word processing fast:

1. Babylon Lounge is a bar in town.
2. Hilary was in Babylon Lounge on Monday.
3. Mum was all dreamy-looking on the phone.

4. Hilary has a phone.
5. Thursday is the day after today.
6. The day after today is Thursday.

My stomach shrinks to the size of a marble.
Mum's got a date.
With Hilary Barnett.
My worst nightmare is coming true.
With knobs on.

10

The Anonymous Note

From then on, my evening is complete and utter pants:

1. When I get back to my bath, the water's gone cool.
2. Mum comes crashing home with a herd of drunken wildebeests, i.e. Man-mad Marge, which means I can't interrogate her about her date.
3. I lie awake in bed for ages wondering how to stop Hilary meeting Mum at the Babylon Lounge, and what's up with Dad, and who nicked my box, and what to wear for my own date on Monday.

By the time I do nod off – *finally* – it's time to make a mad panic dash for school.

Which is the usual riot of joy and laughter . . . not.

For a start, none of my so-called mates are in their Operation Backup positions. Then, in the corridor on my way to Drama with Dex, I turn a corner and slam, slap-bang, into Tonya.

I jump. Dex screams. And Tonya grabs my shoulders

in a bone-crushing grip.

'I've bin finking, right,' she says, shaking me so hard my fillings practically jump out of my teeth. 'I bin finking . . . sticking your *!**!!* ugly head down the toilet ain't gonna do it, yeah? So I've bin talking to my mates, right – my mates from Stonebridge . . .'

Dex makes a gulping noise.

'And they're gonna bang you up bad and I'm gonna film it on my phone.'

And so saying, she shoves me back hard against the wall and stomps off, *clomp, clomp, clomp*, down the corridor.

'Bloody hell!' gasps Dex as Tonya's huge bulk disappears from view. I struggle to get some air back in my lungs. 'B-l-o-o-d-y hell!'

Just then Nat comes tearing round the corner, her shortish brown hair looking even more like an explosion than usual. The second she sees me, her skinny legs jerk to a stop.

'What happened? What's wrong?'

Dex starts to gabble. 'Tonya says she's not going to flush Lozzie's head down the toilet. She says she's gonna get that gang of 16- to 20-year-olds she goes round with from the Stonebridge estate to do something much, much worse.'

At this Nat's pale face goes as white as her shirt and a whimpering sound fills the air.

The whimpering is coming from me.

After that I'm so jittery it's a wonder I'm not carted off to the loony hospital. When the bell goes for Religious Studies, I yelp. When Davina Krackler taps me on the shoulder in the lunch queue, I shriek. And by home-time I have a headache of *global* proportions. Which isn't helped by the fact that Tonya and Fran have spent the entire day watching me. *Intently.*

'I can't take much more of this,' I wail as the gang stick to me like stalkers on the way to the bus stop.

Ems puts her arm around my shoulders.

'It's OK,' she says. The four of them are swapping worried looks. 'At least that Stonebridge lot never hang out round your way. It's too far out.'

'That's true,' adds Nat, keeping her beadies peeled.

'And remember,' chips in Tasha, 'you've still got your date with Oh-My-God-He's-So-Gorgeous Lee.'

At this Ems sighs dreamily, Dex goes to say something but bites it back, and Nat starts singing 'D'ya Think I'm Sexy', which makes everyone laugh including a passing old lady who seems to be wearing a curled-up cat on her head.

By now the five of us are almost at the bus stop. I yank Tasha's sleeve.

'You are *sure* there's nothing going on between Lee and that red-haired girl from St Bernadettes, yeah?'

Tasha rolls her eyes. 'Yeah. I told you, I saw her last night in McDonald's. Her eyes were puffy from crying, she was rubbing a stick-on *I Heart Lee* tattoo off her arm, and her mate was going, "He's not worth it". Look, forget about her and think what you're gonna wear for your date on Monday. I reckon your new Topshop boots and blue denim skirt.'

'With your cream crochet cardigan,' adds Ems enthusiastically.

Tasha splutters. 'A cardigan? On a date? Don't be mental! Wear a tight, low-cut top like a normal person.'

By now the bus has pulled into the stop, and as I'm stepping on board and panicking about tight-fitting tops, a spine chilling thought pops into my head: Suppose Mum's Babylon Lounge date goes so well, she heads straight back to Hilary's house to do . . . stuff?

I go, *'Nnngh'*; Dex goes, 'What?' and as we sit down I hiss in his ear, 'We've got to go to the salon on the way to yours.'

'How come?'

'To stop Hilary and Mum from doing-the-do.'

'Oh. Right. God. *Oh, God!* Gross.'

The ride back takes centuries, mainly because the bus breaks down halfway along Marine Parade and we have to get off and wait twenty minutes for another one to show up. All the time we're travelling and waiting, I think about what I'm going to say to persuade Mum to cancel her date with Hilary. But when I get to the salon, there's no sign of her anywhere: my heart shrivels up like a crisp packet in an oven. In fact, only Kelly and Lucy are in. Kelly is standing in front of one of the mirrors admiring herself in a cool pair of designer jeans, and Lucy's out back doing something on the computer. (All the salon girls use the computer for personal stuff, even though they're not supposed to.)

The minute Lucy sees me, she leans in through the connecting doorway, smiles and says, 'Your mum's got a date so she left early to get her nails done in town. And Christelle's just gone home in a taxi with a bad stomach ache.'

'Did Mum say anything about her date?' I say hopefully – no idea why I'm asking.

Lucy shakes her head and disappears into the back room. Kelly adds, 'Let's hope it's a hot one.' And Dex says, 'Are those designer jeans fake, Kelly?'

That does it. Kelly explodes.

'No, they're bloody well not fake, you little nobby-nobody. They cost me a hundred and twenty quid!'

Out of the corner of my eye I can see Dex's shoulders shaking with laughter. Out back Lucy's scooping up a bunch of envelopes from the salon's out-tray. She plonks a mobile phone on top of the envelope pile and calls out, 'Lauren, any chance you could post these new price lists on your way home, and give your mum back her phone?'

Nodding tightly, I grab the envelopes and phone from her outstretched hand, and signal to Dex to bolt for the door.

Back out on the street, tears of hilarity stream from his eyes.

'*Nobby-nobody*? I ask you! What kind of a plank-brain insult is that?'

He's still laughing as we set off up the High Street, towards his house, past the alley between the bakery and Woolworths. And that's when disaster strikes – yet again. Just as I'm wailing, 'Now I can't even *ring* Mum,' a mad dog shoots out in front of me, right across my path, and next thing – *Oooof!* I'm lying facedown on the pavement, the envelopes scattered like confetti, my skirt up round my bum.

For a second Dex stares at me like I've just morphed into a poodle. Then someone barks his name – me – and he snaps to attention.

'You OK?' he asks, collecting up Mum's phone and the envelopes.

'Hmm, let me see,' I fume, scrambling to my feet. 'My palms are bleeding, my knees are grazed and my knickers have just been seen by the entire world. Oh yes, I'm absolutely marvellous, thank you!'

'Oh. Right. Er . . . so, now is probably not the best time to show you *this*?'

And so saying, he hands me one of the scattered envelopes.

It's addressed to Mr B.

To Mr Hilary B.

To the same Mr Hilary B who's:

1. As bald as a bap, and
2. Has no need for Mum's new salon price list!

Instantly all thoughts of cuts and grazes vanish from my head and my brain is Action-Stations-Go.

Dex leans in and half whispers, 'We could run back to mine and steam the envelope open?'

'Or,' I whisper back, 'we could open it right here, right now and type up another one later.'

For a minute neither of us moves. Then, quick as a

wotsit, I slide my thumb under the flap on the back of the envelope and rip the envelope open.

Inside is a note.

A typewritten, anonymous, blackmail note.

Someone at the salon is threatening Mr Barnett.

The big question is . . . who?

11

Blackmail, She Wrote

Three times Dex and I read the note:

On Monday 19 June go to the High Street and leave the £10,000 in a big brown enveloppe under the paper recycling bin that is next to the Woolworths. Do this at 1 pm and leave the area immediately. If you do not do everything exactly as I say, I go to the police and tell them what I know.

'Sounds like this isn't the first time the blackmailer's been in touch with Hilary,' Dex suggests at last.

'How do you mean?'

'The note doesn't tell him *why* he's being blackmailed. That means the blackmailer must've already sent him a letter saying that he, or *she*, knows his secret, and how much it's gonna cost him to keep her quiet.'

I nod my head slowly, letting this sink in. Then Dex bursts out, 'We need a couple of Cokes to help us think this through!' And before you can say 'the plot thickens', we're legging it back the way we came, down the High Street to The Diner.

The café is more cram packed than a holiday suitcase. Dex slides into the only free booth, nearest the door, and I check out the booth behind, for obvious reasons. Mercifully, the only people sitting there are a bunch of builders and they're too busy talking football to take any notice of us.

I slide onto the seat across the table from Dex, he slides the envelopes and Mum's phone across the table to me, and I am just propping the blackmail note up against the ketchup bottle so we can both see it when he drops a bombshell.

'You know that envelope you delivered to Hilary's on Saturday?'

'Yeah.'

'Well, suppose that wasn't something lovey-dovey from your mum like you were thinking? Suppose *that* was the blackmailer's first note, the one saying she's on to him and has got something incriminating of his that he'll want back?'

My eyeballs go the size of dinosaur eggs. '*NO!*' Then: 'You think? Oh Nelly.' I rake a hand through my hair. 'I hope that doesn't make me a wotsit to the crime, you know . . . What's the word? . . . An accessory.'

Dex is now sitting back in his seat, hand to chin, brain whirring. If he'd had a beard he'd probably have been stroking it.

'You know what else?' he says, at last.

'What?'

'If that envelope you delivered *was* the blackmailer's first note, then Hilary must think you're the blackmailer.'

'*WHAT?*'

'He *saw* you deliver the note from his front window, remember?'

'Aw, *c'mon, Dex!* Be sensible! What kind of idiot hand-delivers an anonymous blackmail note? You'd have to be a right moron to do that.'

'Which is exactly what Hilary thinks you are.'

He has a point. Once, at the school fête, when Mr B was serving coffees and I went up to get one, he said, 'Black or white?' and I said, 'What other colours've you got?' and he went to say, 'You really are a moron, aren't you, Lauren?' but he stopped himself halfway through.

Hmm.

'And another thing!' Dex pushes the blackmail note towards me and points at the word *enveloppe*. 'Dodgy spelling. If the note you delivered had spelling as bad as this, Hilary's bound to think you're the prime suspect.'

'All right,' I accept, at last. 'Let's say you've sussed it and Hilary thinks it's me blackmailing him. What then?'

'*What then?* C'mon, Loz! This isn't exactly a Patricia Cornwell plot.'

This from a boy who thinks Botox is a rude disease!

'If Hilary thinks you're the blackmailer, then it must've been him who ransacked your room, looking for the incriminating thing you've got on him.'

'But I haven't got any incriminating thing on him.'

'*I* know that, but Hilary doesn't, does he?'

It takes me a moment – or ten – to get my head round this.

'*Soooo,* what you're saying is, when Hilary couldn't find what he was looking for in my room, he took my padlocked box reckoning it might be in there.'

'Exactly! He was off sick the afternoon your box was nicked, yeah? And he knew about your spare key because he'd seen your mum getting it out from under the geranium pot when he used to drop her home.'

Blimey! You've got to hand it to Hercule; when his little grey cells work, they work!

Just then Mrs F comes beetling over to tell us she's too busy to make anything to eat but yes, OK, we can have a Coke each provided we don't spend all day drinking it.

After she's huffed off, Dex turns the blackmail note right-side up (he'd turned it face down on the table to hide it from his mum). As he's turning, he gives me a look as if to say, *Why is there now ketchup on this crucial bit of evidence, Lauren?* Then he digs about in his backpack.

'Right!' he announces, pulling out a pad of paper, a pen and a ruler. 'Time to work out the identity of the blackmailer! Let's start with everyone who has access to the salon's post tray.'

As he writes the word SUSPECTS in capital letters and underlines it twice, my brain boots up.

'Hold on!' I blurt loudly. 'If Hilary thinks I'm black-mailing him, how come he's asked Mum out on a date? Why would he want to be dating his blackmailer's mum?'

Dex glances up from his pad. On a separate sheet of paper he's written SUSPECTS' CONNECTION TO HILARY.

'Er . . . not sure,' he says, underlining his heading. 'Maybe he wants to pump her for information about your movements, so he knows where to corner you on your own.'

'Thanks, Dex. You're a big comfort.'

'I'm only saying . . .'

His voice trails off as Mrs F heads over with our drinks. As she zigzags her way between the central tables, she glances down at Ed who's sitting alone, his nose stuck in *The Karate Killer's Handbook*.

'It'd be nice if you asked your brother to join you,' she says wistfully, placing two cans of Coke on our table.

I glare *No way* at Dex; he says, 'No way, Mum,' and Mrs F sighs and moves off to serve another table.

'Finally!' mutters Dex impatiently. 'Now, who uses the salon's post tray? First, there's your mum.'

As he writes *Mrs C* under the word SUSPECTS, a vision of Mum pops into my head. Followed by one of Hilary. Thinking about the two of them makes me break out into a cold sweat. Dex plunges on, unaware.

'Then there's Kelly.'

As he writes her name underneath Mum's, I prop the blackmail note back up against the ketchup bottle.

'Then Lucy.'

And as I'm propping, I start to re-read.

'And Christelle.'

And as I read, something sparks in my brain.

'Anyone else?'

It's like there's an electric current in my head . . .

'Loz?'

But it keeps cutting out.

'LOZZIE!'

I snap to attention. 'What?'

'I said, does anyone else work at the salon other than your mum, Kelly, Lucy and Christelle?'

'Er . . . no. Only Cathy. The cleaner.'

'Cathy,' he murmurs, adding her name to his list. 'Is that spelt with a C or a K?'

I roll my eyes and go back to reading the note.

'OK. Let's start with your mum. Now, we know she's having her nails done for her date with Hilary . . .'

There's something about this note that isn't right.

' . . . which she probably wouldn't do if she was black-mailing him.'

Something about the way it *sounds* . . .

'Then there's Kelly.'

The door to the café bangs open, making me jump.

'She's just bought herself some really expensive jeans . . .'

Three men in suits are standing in the doorway.

' . . . which, I bet, she couldn't've afforded on her wages.'

Suddenly Mrs F is by our side.

'Come on, you two. I need this table,' she says, beckoning to the three suits in the doorway. 'Go on home now – to your own homes, mind – and get on with your homework.'

'But Mum!' Dex looks outraged. 'We're in the middle of something *vital.*'

'I don't care.' Mrs F has her arms crossed tightly. 'Go home and get on with your homework. Oh, and take Ed with you.'

Muttering darkly, Dex shoves his pen, pad and ruler into his backpack. Saying thanks for the Coke, I scoop the blackmail note, Mum's envelopes and phone into my bag. Then, like prisoners in a chain-gang, the two of us shuffle past The Suits and out onto the High Street.

Where we are joined by Ed.

Wearing a black woollen balaclava.

In June.

'Is there a particular reason for the knitted guerrilla mask, do you think?' I ask Dex in a low voice.

'You mean besides letting the entire street know I'm related to total freaking embarrassment?'

'Don't despair.' I give him a sympathetic squeeze. 'The alien spaceship *will* return and take him back, one day.'

Walking along – Ed at our heels, scanning the rooftops, for snipers – Dex and I say nothing. If balaclava-boy overheard even the faintest whisper of anything to do with blackmail, he'd have our phones bugged, seriously. When we get to Park Road, which is my turning for home, Dex says meaningfully, 'Talk later, yeah?' Then, dropping his voice: 'Kelly could easily've bought those jeans on a credit card, knowing she'll soon have £10,000 to pay off the bill.'

It's gone five o'clock by the time I get in. Karen's not home (Hallelujah!) so I whop on some loud music, change out of my uniform into my combat shorts, and wander out into the back garden. On one side of the fence, mad Mr Peterson is trimming his lawn with a pair of nail scissors. On the other, Mrs Greenidge is singing hymns. I go back in. There is only so much weirdness one girl can take.

Back inside, up in my room, staring at the blackmail note on my desk, a zillion thoughts go banging round my head. *Could Kelly be the blackmailer? What's the link between her and Hilary? What is this thing that he has done? And what is it about this note that's soooo bugging me?*

By now my brain is going scrambly, so I roll my neck to stop a headache from coming on then stretch my arms in the air. As I'm stretching, I glance down at yesterday's half-finished French homework, which is lying next to the note. It reads:

Task 1. Write a letter to a French pen pal telling them about yourself, your likes and your dislikes.

And underneath that I've written:

Cher Pen pal
Bonjor. Je m'appelle Lozzie. J'ai quatorze ans.
J'aime la musique et le chocolat chaud et les
Jaffa...

And that's when it hits me.

Oh, Nelly!

Good God!

I know who the blackmailer is!

I grab the note, fly downstairs and punch in Dex's number. He picks up and before he's even halfway through saying, 'Hello?' I splurt out, 'Kelly's not the blackmailer!'

Pause.

'How do you know?'

'Listen to this and tell me how it *sounds*.'

Slowly, clearly, I read out the blackmail note.

'Well, the whole thing sounds a bit . . . er . . .'

'Clunky?'

'Yeah, clunky. Stilted. Clumsy.'

'*Exactly!* It sounds like it's been translated into English from another language. Take that bit about Woolworths. We'd just say "next to Woolworths", yeah? Only someone who speaks another language, say, one where they put *le* or *la* in front of words, would say "next to *the* Woolworths".'

It takes Hercule a minute or two to get his little grey cells around what I'm saying. Then I can practically hear his jaw crash through his hallway floor.

'*Christelle? No!* It can't be! But why?'

12

The Buried Body

I can't see Dex's face, for obvious reasons, but my guess is it looks like it did that time he got up in Assembly to report on a school chess match and when he sat back down Nat told him his trousers were undone. Which they weren't.

'Christelle?' he repeats. 'Christelle!'

There is a pause while I wait for him to say something else, something brilliant, but instead all I hear is a frantic, 'Bugger! That's Dad coming in. Call you later.'

And with that, *click*, he's gone.

He still hasn't called back by the time I go to bed. Or by the time Mum comes home from her date (alone, thank God). She tiptoes up the stairs, taps gently on Karen's door, then on mine and pokes her head round the frame.

'You awake?' she whispers.

I turn on my side, facing the door, and switch on the bedside light. One glance at her face and my heart sinks. She looks so *happy*. Happier than she has done in ages. Like she's won the Lottery or something. I want to splurt, *Oh, Mum, no! He hates me.* But instead all I say is, 'D'you have a good time?' And when she beams, 'Love-ly,' I say, fighting tears, 'Great. Night-night then,' and snap off my light.

For what seems like for ever, she stands in the door-way, watching me, I guess. Then she comes over and stroking my hair, says softly, 'Night-night, my little prickly pear. Sleep tight.'

Which, of course, I don't.

The last thing I think about before I nod off is her big, happy starry-eyed smile. And in my dreams, I panic about how she's going to react when she discovers that the new love of her life is a burglar and – possibly – worse.

★ ★ ★

I snap awake. The sky is dark, the house is still and there's a ringing sound coming from the corner of my room! For a split second I can't work out what's hap-pening. Then it hits me: the ringing is coming from my school bag. I jump out of bed and reach my mobile just in time. The whispering voice on the line is recognis-able instantly.

'Loz, listen! I think I know why Christelle's black-mailing Hilary!'

I glance at my alarm clock. 12.15. *AM!*

Still on my knees, I shuffle across to the edge of my bed, phone to ear, and shove my head under the duvet.

'Dex, do you *want* to be murdered by your dad?' I hiss.

'It's OK. No one will hear. The lights are off and they're all upstairs asleep.'

I have a vision of Dex standing in his unlit hallway in his underpants. I shake my head to make the vision go away.

He steams on excitedly, 'Christelle's a hairdresser, right? And your mum says clients often open up to hairdressers and tell them things, personal things, things that they might not tell someone else?'

This is a fact. One time Mum was cutting a new client's hair and the woman confided that she'd had a sex change operation!

Dex carries on, 'Well, suppose one of Christelle's clients let slip something to her about *Hilary* . . .'

'Like what?'

'Like something to do with his wife's leaving. She left really suddenly, you know. *Really* suddenly. I asked Mum a few "casual" questions when she got home – she knows someone who knows Hilary's neighbour – and she said actually Mrs Barnett's leaving did cause a bit of a stir because, and I'm quoting, "It's like she disappeared without a trace."'

'So, what are you saying? Christelle heard about Hilary's wife leaving and thought, I wonder if he's murdered her and buried her up on the Downs. Hey, I know! I'll blackmail him on the off-chance and see if he pays up?'

'It's a possibility.'

'Tell you what's also a possibility.'

'What?'

'You watch too much TV!'

'Think about it, Loz! Christelle must hear loads of gossip every week. She could be blackmailing other clients or neighbours of clients too.'

'Are you *serious*?'

'Have you still got those envelopes with the salon's price lists?'

'Yes.'

'Well, don't post them yet. Open them and check what's inside.'

Check what's inside?

I'm just about to ask him if he's forgotten just how many of those envelopes there are when this happens: down the phone line comes an ear-splitting karate cry. Then a heart-stopping *AAARGH!* Then an almighty clattering and thud like the sound of a receiver and a body slamming to the ground.

I don't believe it! The karate freak has floored Dex! I listen in, agog.

'GET OFF ME . . . ED!'

Ooof . . . Yeow . . . Thud!

'BOG OFF, YOU . . .'

Ooof!

'MUTANT!'

CRASH!

'DEXTER! EDWARD! WHAT THE ★★★★! . . .?'

'It wasn't me, Dad. It was Dex. He was using the phone. Again.'

'I'll deal with you in the morning, Dexter. Now get up those stairs, the both of you. I said, up those stairs. NOW.'

After the receiver has been smashed down, I pull my head back out from under my duvet and fume. Why does Mr F always side with the freak in the family? Why does he always pick on Dex? It's exactly the same with Mum. Only last week she went completely bonker-satronic at me for having her lip liner sharpener in my pencil-case when it wasn't even me who'd borrowed it in the first place. It was Karen. I'd taken it from *her* room.

Still fuming, I climb into bed, yank the duvet up over my shoulder and screw my eyes into little fists. Five seconds later they're wide open again and I'm staring into the dark. And the more I stare, the more I think. And what I'm thinking is: Could Dex be right? Could Christelle have overheard something sinister at the salon? My brain starts to whirr. OK, so it's possible: Christelle could have heard about Mr B's wife, decided to spy on him and then secretly filmed him bundling her body into the boot of his car or digging her grave on the Downs. But how likely is that? And even if she did, why didn't she go straight to the police? I know she isn't always the sanest person on the planet – once she put up photos of her ex-boyfriend in his neighbour-hood with the caption, *Don't trust this man* – but surely she wouldn't do something as serious as blackmail unless there was a really good *personal* reason?

I roll onto my side and stare at the wall.

And another thing. If Hilary did murder his wife, how come no one's found the body? In films, people are always stumbling across dead bodies buried in the woods: they're out with their dog; the dog paws the ground; the camera zooms in and there it is, the missing corpse – eyes open wide, jaw twisted in terror, maggots feeding on the rotting . . .

I snap on my light.

Oh, Nelly! Now I'm freaking myself out!

I leap out of bed, scurry over to my school bag and root through the envelopes for this month's copy of *Rebel,* to get rid of the creeps.

And that's when I remember the second part of Dex's theory.

B-l-o-o-d-y Nora! Could he be right? Could Christelle really be blackmailing someone else as well?

13

Nat's Brain Boots Up

Next morning (Friday) I sleep through my alarm. Which means I have to rush, rush, rush for the bus. Which means I only just manage to fling myself on board as the driver is pulling away from the stop.

'What in the name of Nora happened to your hair?' asks Dex, who has saved me a seat at the back. 'Why is it so frizzy?'

'It's frizzy,' I explain, straining not to hit him, 'because that's what happens to hair when you spend half the night standing over a boiling kettle steaming open envelopes.'

His eyes light up like Wembley Stadium. 'Did you find more blackmail notes? Is Christelle blackmailing anyone else?'

I shoot him my *murderers-rapists-Karen* look.

'Oh! . . . Shame!' Then: 'Why didn't you rip the envelopes open and type up new ones this morning? You should've typed up new ones, you know. That would've been much quicker.'

I press my lips together and make a smacking sound.

'And do you not *think* I'd have done that if I'd *had* thirty-five envelopes to hand?'

He makes a face like *Ah!* 'There were *thirty-five* envelopes?'

'O-o-h, yes.'

'And it takes what? About three minutes to steam each envelope?'

'Yes, again.'

'So we're talking . . . er . . . an hour and twenty minutes of steaming?'

'Uh-huh!'

'Blimey! No wonder your hair looks like a frizz ball.'

I don't do a lot of talking on the bus ride in – partly because Dex is so full of his Buried Body theory I can't get a word in edgewise, but mainly because I'm too tired, depressed and stressed: tired from the steam thing; depressed from the Mum thing; and stressed at the thought of Tonya and her Stonebridge mates hanging about outside school waiting to mash me to mincemeat. I send Ems a panicky text: *U r at bus stop, rite?* to check she hasn't forgotten, then force myself to take some deep breaths. After that I plaster my hair with Mum's *De-frizz Ease* and smooth every last strand back into a ponytail.

Incredibly, Ems, Nat *and* Tash are all standing at the stop when the bus pulls up. As soon as they see me, they stop glancing nervously over their shoulders and grin and wave like loonies. Not for the first time since the week began, my eyes prickle.

'Calm yourselves, ladies!' shouts Dex, stepping off the

bus. 'There's only one of me to go round.'

Nat gives him a slap across the back of the head and links her arm through mine.

'You can't take any chances with that Stonebridge lot,' she says firmly.

'They could be hiding anywhere,' adds Ems, intently.

Tash nods stiffly and takes my other arm, but not before glancing at my hair.

I can feel my bottom lip trembling; my eyes are filling up.

'You really are top mates,' I say, blinking back tears. 'The best. I don't know what I'd do without you.'

And I don't. Truly.

Ems juts out her bosoms.

'C'mon!' she rallies. 'We'll show that Stonebridge mob who's scared!'

And off we stride, chins up, chests out, like generals marching to war, until Tash gasps, 'Oh God, is that them?' then we run like demented chickens.

Later, we realise the two 'yobs' Tash was gasping about can't have been from the Stonebridge gang because:

1. They were old enough to be our dads;
2. They looked like startled rabbits as we stampeded by.

All of which prompts Dex to point out that it might be helpful if at least one of us knew what the Stonebridge gang members look like exactly, so we know who we're supposed to be running from.

By now the bell has gone and we're on route to our first lesson of the day: Physics followed by Physics. Nice.

On the way to class, we pass Lee Quick in the corridor. As he strolls past, our hands brush together (his and mine) and my insides judder like a juggernaut.

'Still OK for Monday?' he calls out, glancing back, casual cool.

'Yeah,' I squeak, tugging my ponytail straight. 'Yeah. Fine.'

And he flashes me the YUMMIEST smile.

Ems turns to slush.

'OhmyGodohmyGodohmyGod!' she gibbers. 'He looks so LUSH when he smiles. His eyes crinkle up and everything.'

I'm still thinking about Lee and his everything when halfway through Physics something jabs me in the back. I snap my head round and find Frank Fabiola passing me a note from Fran. It says: *Don't think coz Tonya aint hear I aint waching u.*

I write back: *Excellent.* Hey, what's the worst she can do? She's a stick insect without backup.

And I have a date with the luscious, luscious Lee!

At breaktime, me and the girls go over the Lee-in-the-Corridor incident moment by moment: the way his dark eyes flashed when he saw me (yum); the way his hand accidentally-on-purpose touched mine (double yum); the way he smiled, with his teeth showing, like a hungry shark (yum, yum, yum, yum, YUM). At one point my cheeks go so red from the thrill of it all, Nat shouts, 'Hose her down; she's about to blow!'

Dex, who has been listening in, is also about to explode. But not from girly excitement.

'Doesn't *anyone* want to hear about Hilary murdering his wife?' he huffs.

That does it. The summit meeting stops, the girls go, '*WHAT?*' and before you can say, 'So that's it on the Lee front, right?' he and I are telling them everything: about me unknowingly delivering the first blackmail note, about Hilary thinking I'm the blackmailer and nicking my box, about Dex and me finding the second blackmail note, about Mum and Hilary going on a date to Babylon Lounge, about Mrs Barnett's 'disappearance', about Christelle being the last person you'd suspect of blackmail, about her coming to stay with us after Mercedes died – *everything*!

When we've finished, the girls blink at us like they've all got blinkeritis. Then Nat and Tash breathe, 'Unbelievable' and Ems says, 'Isn't Mercedes a type of car?'

Just then Mrs Niblock leans out of a second floor window and bellows: 'Why aren't you five out on the playing field? The bell went fifteen minutes ago.'

And so for the second time that morning we do our demented chicken run, first to the changing rooms, then out on to the rounders field where Mr Frazer (our PE teacher) gives us a rollicking so nuclear, it's a miracle his shouting doesn't start an avalanche.

Surprisingly, given the rubbish start, rounders turns out to be great fun. Ems bowls like a demon; I catch Mr Frazer out at first post; and Fran accidentally whacks herself on the back of the head with the bat while trying to impress Mickey Finn. As I say to the girls in the changing rooms afterwards, if it weren't for Mum doing-the-do with a murderer and me being on a gang's hit list, I could die happy.

After PE, it's a quick shower and change and off to the cafeteria for lasagne, chips and peas. *Dee-lish*. Nat bags us some seats at a table near the door and she and Dex sit on one side, facing the door, with Tash, Ems and me on the other. After a bit, Dex tips his chair back on two legs so that he can talk to Pete Ray at the table behind, and Nat leans forward and whispers, 'Do you really think Christelle would blackmail someone she didn't know just for the money?'

I whisper back, 'No. I've been thinking about that and I can't believe she'd be so cold-hearted and . . .'

I break off as Dex's chair comes crashing back forward.

Just then Ems nudges me in the ribs and jerks her head back a bit in the direction of the door. I swivel my own head, thinking: Oh, Nelly! Please don't let it be Tonya. It'd be so typical of her to turn up to school in time for a feed.

But it isn't Tonya. It's Hilary. And he looks *dreadful*. His face is as pale as a maggot, his shirt is only half ironed, and the circles under his eyes are dark like a bruise.

'That's the look of guilt, that is,' whispers Tash and I nod, thinking: How come he looks *this* bad when he's just had such a brilliant date with Mum?

Hawk-like, we watch him as he circles round the tables to the head of the lunch queue.

From across the room Frankie Boyle shouts out, 'Rough night, Sir?'

But Hilary doesn't shoot him down with a glare or try to crush the laughter. He simply picks up his lunch and walks back to the exit. As he approaches, I move my chair to get a better look and it makes a loud scraping noise on the floor. Like an animal caught in headlights, his head snaps round. But instead of fixing me with the evil eye, which you'd think he would seeing as how he suspects I'm blackmailing him, he blanks me, totally. It's like he's not aware I'm there.

After he's gone, my whole body shudders like it's been dunked in an ice bucket.

Nat fixes me with a penetrating look.

'Are you sure Christelle's never said *anything* to you that might make you think she knows Hilary personally?'

Dex squints at Nat as if to say, *What's that got to do with him killing his wife?* and Ems and Tash look confused.

I shake my head. 'The only time Christelle ever mentioned Hilary to me was at Mum's party. She said she'd read his novel; I said, did she know it was written by my teacher, and she'd said yes and looked away.'

Nat turns up the heat. 'What do you mean? "Looked away", how?'

'Like talking about him and his book was making her uncomfortable.'

'I expect she was feeling guilty about the blackmail,' chips in Ems.

Tash nods and Dex takes off his glasses and starts wiping them slowly.

Nat frowns. 'Did the novel get mentioned again when you met up at The Diner?'

I crank my mind back to Tuesday afternoon. 'No. All she said was, she was sorry about my box getting nicked and she was expecting some dosh, enough to buy a flat . . .'

Then I realise. *Of course!* The money Christelle was expecting – she was expecting to blackmail it from Hilary!

I open my mouth to say this out loud and something goes *Zing!* in my brain. I let out a gasp.

'I've just remembered!' I splurt. 'About the money . . .'

Dex puts his glasses back on quickly.

'Christelle said it had something to do with Mercedes.'

Nat presses, '*What* to do with Mercedes?'

'She said something like . . . the dosh belonged to Mercedes or was owed to Mercedes. Yeah, that's it! She said the dosh she was expecting "*should've gone*" to Mercedes.'

Dex's eyes lock onto mine. 'Those were her exact words?' I nod. 'What else did she say?'

'Er . . . she talked about Mercedes: about how much she missed her, about how she'd sorted through all her stuff after she'd died . . . about how she'd packed up all her gear in the flat.'

Nat shoots forward on her chair.

'Here's an idea,' she says conspiratorially. We all lean in, ears on stalks. 'Suppose it wasn't *Christelle* who started this whole blackmail business. Suppose it was *Mer-*

cedes who first got hold of something incriminating about Hilary and was using it to blackmail him for something he'd done to her. Then, after she died, Christelle found this "thing" while she was packing up Mercedes stuff and, to take revenge for her friend, took over the blackmail.'

For a moment no one says a word. Then: 'Of course!' I exclaim. Tash almost shoots out of her chair. 'If Christelle's first blackmail note, the one I delivered, made it obvious to Hilary that he was being blackmailed by someone who knew Mercedes and had access to her stuff, that would explain why he's so sure I'm the blackmailer! He knows Mum was mates with Mercedes because he'd seen them together in his class, so he must've reckoned I knew Mercedes through Mum.'

Dex looks at me then at Nat then back at me.

'You know what else it explains?' he says quietly. 'It explains why Hilary looked so furious after he'd overheard you and Christelle in The Diner. Up until then he can't've known Mercedes had a flatmate. Up until then he had no idea that the person blackmailing him isn't you, but Christelle.'

14

Fran, a Plan and Deep, Deep Trouble

'Britain had begun to prepare for the Second World War long before Germany's invasion of Poland . . .'

Back in class after lunch, listening but not listening, I slip Dex a note. It says: *We've got to tell Christelle her cover is blown.*

He writes back: *Will she be at the salon after school?* And I nod yes.

Just then Mrs Hutchin turns to face the blackboard and I swivel my head in Nat's direction . . . and lock eyeballs with Fran.

I glare at her. She glares at me. And Mrs Hutchin pumps up the volume.

'Of course, the British public never knew when the enemy might strike . . .'

Fran's lips curve into a faint smile.

'They never knew when the German bombers might attack.'

The smile is now full-on evil and nasty.

My stomach clenches. My throat goes tight. Oh, Nelly! If only I hadn't pressed that stupid *Reply All* key! If only I hadn't emailed that picture of Tonya to the entire class.

I am still wishing I could time travel back a week when the final bell goes.

'I'd like a quick word, Lauren,' calls out Mrs Hutchin, shifting her bottom off her desk.

Miserably, I shamble up to the front and stare at the holiday brochure poking out of her bag. If there's one thing guaranteed about a Mrs Hutchin 'quick word', it's:

1. Never quick.
2. Never just *a* word.
3. Never includes the phrase, 'Your coursework was a delight to read, Lauren.'

I wait patiently while she explains something about me doing History at GCSE. (Outside the window Nat is doing an excellent impersonation of Old Retardo.) Then she says something about me needing to pull my socks up concentration-wise. (Nat's impression is bloody funny.) Then she says something else – no idea what – and I shuffle my feet a bit and say, 'Yes . . . thanks . . . thanks very much,' and dash into the grounds to join the others.

Outside the school railings, across the street, Fran is watching the five of us closely. With one hand she flicks her tragically thin hair; in the other, she holds her phone.

'Probably waiting for the zoo to ring to say there's room for her in the giraffe house,' says Tash, which makes us laugh; Fran is freakishly tall.

All of a sudden Ems grabs my shoulder.

'What if she's waiting to ring Tonya to tell her we're on our way to the bus stop?' she gabbles, eyes wide. 'What if the Stonebridge lot are lurking near the alleyway right now?'

'Then we'll just have to take the side entrance and go the long way round,' cuts in Dex quickly.

Ems eyes are now as big as a baby's. 'But what if they catch us up? They could have cars, you know. That Stonebridge lot nick cars.'

Again I get that stomach-going-down-too-fast-in-a-lift feeling. There's a strong chance I'm going to be sick.

Tash cruises in.

'No worries,' she says calmly, like we're discussing the price of sausages over a cup of tea. 'I'll tell her there's a call for her in the office. I'll say . . .' There is a pause while Tash's brain revs up. 'I'll say . . . it's some photographer who spotted her this morning on his way to a job. She'll think she's heading straight for the cover of *Loaded* and will be up those stairs fast as hell.'

Dex rolls his eyes and scoffs, 'Aw, c'mon Tash. Don't be a teacake! Only someone with a brain the size of a Brussels sprout would fall for that!'

And he's right. Only someone with a brain the size of a Brussels sprout *would* fall for that.

Which explains why Fran goes for it, big-time.

★ ★ ★

One bloody long sprint and a bus ride later, Dex and I are back on the High Street, heading for the salon.

'Slow down, dude,' I call, as Dex does his power walk thing again. 'The salon doesn't close 'til six. Christelle will still be there.'

But, as it turns out, Christelle isn't still there.

'I could tell she hadn't fully recovered from her stomach bug when she came in this morning,' says Mum, snipping away at some man's hair, 'so I told her to go home after lunch. Why? What did you want to see her about?'

I wrack my brains for a lie.

Dex leaps in, 'We need some help with a project we're doing. A French project . . .'

I interrupt, 'Yeah.'

'And we need Christelle's help.'

The snipping stops and Mum's eyes squint at mine in the mirror. Then she sighs and says, 'Well, Christelle can't help you at the moment, so please don't even *think* about going round there.'

Christelle's flat is on the top floor of a long, red-bricked block with an open-air staircase leading to each level, and concrete walkways leading to the flats' front doors. On the way over there, my brain is freaking out with *what ifs*: What if Christelle is so furious I opened her blackmail note she refuses ever to speak to me again? What if the police find out what she's been doing and throw her in prison? What if now Hilary knows she's the blackmailer he comes looking for her?

By the time we get to Christelle's block, my head is

so cluttered up with nightmare visions it's a wonder I can find the staircase that leads to her flat. We take the steps two at a time to the top floor, turn left on to her walkway and hurry along to her front door.

Which is standing half open, the pane of glass nearest the lock smashed in.

For a second Dex and I look at each other, not breathing. Then I call out, 'Hey, Christelle. It's me. Loz. Hello.'

No answer.

I take a deep breath and push the door open wide. Then I step inside, heart jumping, listening for noises.

Nothing.

I inch a bit further down the short, wooden floored hallway, and am just thinking about turning back when I feel breath on the back of my neck. I spin round, there is a scream, and my heart rockets into space.

'DEX, you ARSE!' I hiss, my heart still hurtling past Mars. 'You stupid, stupid ARSE!'

By now I'm sweating like a boxer. I drag my shirt sleeve across my forehead, wait for my breathing to slow down, then carry on inching, Dex close behind.

To the left of us is a tiny bathroom, its door open all the way. To the right, a kitchen, its door almost closed. I suck in another breath, push the kitchen door open properly and peek in.

Nothing.

I do the same at the next door: a tidy bedroom with a double bed. And at the next: another bedroom with a single bed. Again there's no sign of Christelle or Hilary.

But the second bedroom has been ransacked. Totally. There are overturned packing boxes on the floor, a pile of box files emptied onto the bed, and an old typewriter sitting undisturbed on the desk.

The hairs on the back of my neck prickle. I glance over my shoulder, and Dex tilts his head in the direction of the final door, which, I'm guessing, leads to the lounge.

Side by side, like Siamese twins, we edge towards the door. Slowly, slowly, we push it open with our feet. And freeze.

This time, there's sign of Christelle, all right.

This time, she's lying sprawled out on the carpet, head slumped to one side, a patch of fresh blood seeping through the back of her hair.

15

Panic Stations Go

'CHRISTELLE!'

I hurl myself across the room, my heart banging so wildly it feels too big for my chest.

'Christelle!' I sob, falling onto my knees beside her. 'Christelle!'

Her eyelids flutter slightly, but she doesn't speak. She just lies there, flat on her back, eyes closed, blood seeping through her lovely bleached blonde hair.

My body is now shaking uncontrollably. On the other side of the lounge I can hear Dex talking rapidly into Christelle's phone.

'What street is this?' he calls out urgently.

My eyes are riveted to the receiver in his hand.

'LOZ! C'MON! What STREET?'

'Hurlock,' I croak, my voice not working properly.

'WHAT FLAT NUMBER?'

'Thirty-three.'

Dex repeats the address down the phone. When he gets off, his face is white.

'The operator says we've gotta get her in the recovery

position.' Instantly he rolls Christelle onto her side like they do on *ER*. 'He said check for her breathing and stop the blood too.'

Blurry-eyed, I look about me. The room has been wrecked! Dex puts his cheek next to Christelle's mouth to check her breathing. In the distance, there is a siren wailing. He shouts, 'Quick! Get a towel!' and I stumble to the bathroom. When I get back, the siren sound is closer. Dex grabs the towel from my shaking hands and presses it to the back of Christelle's head. The siren noise is getting nearer. The siren is now on top of us.

'Is she breathing OK?' I whisper hoarsely.

Dex looks up at me and says shakily, 'I – I think so.'

Just then two paramedics come hurrying into the room, followed soon after by two police officers.

'Do you know what happened?' asks one of the medics.

'No,' says Dex, scrambling to his feet. 'The door was open and we just found her.'

Medic 1: 'What's her name?'

Dex: 'Christelle.'

Medic 2: 'Is she diabetic, epileptic, allergic to any-thing?'

Dex: 'I'm not sure.'

Then me, stammering: 'N-n-n-o. No. I don't think so.'

After that, the medics get to work and the police offi-cers take Dex and I aside. The woman PC ushers me into the tidy bedroom, sits me down and asks me ques-tions; the man PC does the same in the kitchen with Dex.

By now Christelle is on a stretcher and the medics are manoeuvring her out of the lounge. 'Can I come in the ambulance with her?' I ask in a tiny voice as they steady the stretcher past the bedroom doorway.

'Best not, love,' comes the reply. 'The police will take you home.'

After the medics have gone, the police ring the salon and The Diner to tell our parents what's happening. Then they check out the flat. While they're looking round the trashed bedroom, I follow Dex, like a lost lamb, into the lounge. He peers at the shelves above the red stain on the carpet. As he's peering, the woman PC comes in.

'There's a bit of blood and hair on there,' he says pointing at the corner of one of the shelves. 'She must've hit her head as she fell.'

The woman PC takes a closer look at the shelf then smiles at Dex. Tightly.

Soon, other people arrive – a fingerprint officer and a police photographer, I guess. Then the two uniformed PCs drive us back to my house, where we've been told my mum and Dex's dad will be waiting.

On the ride over Dex whispers, 'Did you tell them anything about the blackmail note?'

I shake my head.

'Did you tell them we reckon it was Hilary that attacked her?'

More head shaking from me.

'Good. Don't say anything to anyone till we've thought this through, yeah?'

I nod. 'OK.'

Back home, Mum is all hugs and sighs of relief that we're safe. Mr F just pats Dex awkwardly on the back.

'You've had a shock, son,' he says, which is, I think, the second longest speech I've ever heard him make. The longest was last year when Dex asked his mum if he could get his ear pierced and Mr F, overhearing, muttered, 'Give me strength! Next he'll be wanting to wear a sarong.'

After cups of tea and the third degree, Dex and his dad go home, and Mum and me sit snuggled together on the sofa.

'Christelle will be fine, you'll see,' she says lightly.

But I can hear the wobble in her voice.

After a bit, there's the crash of the front door being flung open and Karen and Dave come galumphing in. Straightaway Mum fills them in on the story so far: Karen looks truly shocked; Dave looks like he can't remember his name. Then we all troop into the kitchen for something to eat – scrambled eggs on toast for us girls; the entire contents of the fridge for Dave.

While we're sitting in the kitchen, talking and eating, Karen's eyes suddenly go the size of a prize tomato.

'Omigod,' she exclaims, clamping her hand to her mouth. 'I've just thought. Christelle won't lose her memory or anything like that, will she?'

Dave stretches back in his chair.

'No! 'Course not, babe,' he drawls, both hands resting on top of his sexy, messed-up hair. 'I was knocked unconscious once and look at me now.'

There is a pause while we all look at Dave.

Holy Moley! It's a miracle the man remembers to breathe.

★ ★ ★

Later that evening, after Dave has gone home, Mum rings the hospital to check on Christelle. Anxiously, Karen and I follow her into the hallway and perch on the stairs.

'The good news is, Christelle's now conscious,' beams Mum, getting off the phone. 'The even better news is she's going to make a full and complete recovery.'

For a nanosecond I stare at Mum, not sure I've heard her right. Then Karen blows out a whoosh of breath and says, 'Thank God,' and I punch the air and roar, '*Yeeeeessssss!*'

After that, the three of us troop upstairs to bed.

'You'll spark out tonight, love, I expect,' coos Mum, standing in my bedroom doorway.

But, oddly enough, she's wrong.

For ages, I sit huddled on my bed, hugging my knees and wondering: what *was* Hilary looking for when he trashed Mercedes's stuff? And whatever it was, did he or didn't he find it?

16

Fears and Tears

Next morning (Saturday) Mum and I set off for the hospital after breakfast – if you can call porridge with skimmed milk and no sugar 'breakfast'.

In the car on the way over, Mum looks really washed-out; her under-eyes are all baggy and she's wearing no makeup. But once inside the hospital, she perks up and marches to the reception desk.

'We're here to see Christelle Saloun,' she says briskly. 'She was admitted yesterday with a head injury.'

'Are you relatives of hers?' asks the receptionist.

'Yes.'

I shoot Mum a look as if to say, *We are?* and the receptionist flicks through some papers. Then he says, 'Christelle Saloun. Ward nine, third floor.' And me and Mum hurry over to the lift.

On the way up to the third floor, Mum gives me a watery smile.

'How come you said we're Christelle's rellys?' I ask.

'Because we are in a way, aren't we? She doesn't have any contact with her real relatives any more, so you,

Karen and I are the nearest thing to a proper family she's got.'

Deep inside I burst out laughing. Imagine coming round after a whack on the head to discover you're related to Karen, Queen of Darkness.

We find Christelle propped up in the nearest bed of a ward full of papery-thin old ladies. As soon as I see her poor bandaged head my heart lurches; she looks so lost and lonely. She tries to force a big smile as we come into the ward, but clearly it's too much for her.

'Sorry,' she sobs. 'Sorry. Sorry.'

And both Mum and me hurry over to comfort her: Mum holds her as gently as a baby, I squeeze her hand.

'How are you feeling?' asks Mum at last, pulling up a chair. I pull up another on the other side of the bed.

Christelle dabs her eyes dry with the edge of her sheet.

'OK,' she says weakly. 'Ze painkillers are working.'

Mum carries on, 'Do you need anything? Want anything?'

Christelle shakes her head and winces with the pain and Mum says, 'Do you remember what happened?'

Immediately my heart speeds up. Christelle takes a deep breath.

'I am at home, ill. I go out to buy some medicine. I come back and find a burglar in ze lounge. I – 'ow you say – confront 'im?' Mum nods. 'We argue. 'e pushes me. I fall backward and all is black.'

There is a short silence. Then Mum asks gently, 'Can you remember what he looked like?'

And I, idiotically, without thinking, blurt out, 'It was Mr Barnett, wasn't it?'

Christelle's eyes open wide like an owl's.

So do Mum's.

'Good God, Lozzie,' she splutters. 'What on earth makes you say that?'

I stare down at my lap. Damn! DAMN! Why did I splurt *that* out in front of Mum? I was going to wait until she went to the loo.

Miserably, I lift my eyes up to Christelle's and in a small voice say, 'Sorry . . . but I know about you black-mailing him.'

At first Christelle stares at me like she's seeing her own ghost. Then her face crumples and a fat tear rolls down her cheek.

Mum puts the boot in, 'Lauren, will you please tell me what is going on?'

But before I can even think where to start, Christelle does something totally unexpected. She sucks in a breath, gives herself a little shake, glances at the old lady wearing headphones in the next bed, then says firmly and clearly, 'Yes, Lauren is right. It waz 'ilary Barnett who pushed me. And yes, I was blackmailing 'im.'

And so saying, she wipes her face with her hands, sucks in another breath and starts to tell her tale.

17

A Tale of Betrayal

By the time Christelle has finished telling her story I'm so stunned, Lee Quick could have tangoed past me in nothing but a pair of earrings and I wouldn't have noticed. And can you wonder given that *this* is what happened: Not long ago, Mum was in the salon raving on about Hilary's new novel and saying how one of its characters reminded her a bit of Christelle. So, even though Christelle isn't big on reading (unless you count *Vogue* as a book) she borrowed Mum's copy of *Haunts of the Black-eyed Girl* and had a flick through. And what she read made her eyeballs almost shoot out of her head. The novel practically told Mercedes's life story! It was full of stuff that had happened to her, and to Christelle, some of it really, *really* personal.

Well, this made Christelle suspicious, big-time. For one thing, she was sure Mercedes would never have confided anything about her private life to someone like Hilary. And for another, she knew Mercedes had been writing a novel on her grandfather's typewriter. So, she did what any sane person would do – she searched through Mercedes's papers to see if she could find the novel she'd been writing. And when she couldn't find that, she practically ripped the flat apart looking for a letter, a note, a diary entry – *anything* that might prove Mercedes had written *Haunts of the Black-eyed Girl* and had shown it to Hilary. It wasn't until there were papers everywhere that she glanced under the sofa in the lounge. And there, inside a folder full of old Valentine's cards and photos and other stuff Mercedes had treasured, she found what she'd been looking for: a cassette tape from the flat's ancient answerphone that had been used for recording incoming messages.

At the mention of the cassette tape, Mum's hand goes over her mouth as if she's guessed what's coming next, and my brain flashes up a picture of Dad's *Thrashers* tape as last I saw it, mangled to bits. Then it hits me: Oh. Dear. Nora. Of course! It must've been Christelle's *answerphone tape* that Hilary was after when he stole my box.

Christelle carries on. Turns out that on this old answerphone tape was a message to Mercedes from Hilary, praising her to the skies for *Haunts of the Black-eyed Girl* and saying how honoured he was to be the first person to read it, and would she like to meet him the following week for a drink so he could return the manuscript and suggest some slight improvements. (But, of course, this meeting never took place because, by Christelle's reckoning, Hilary must've left his message sometime between Tuesday the second and Saturday the fifth of November, and Mercedes died on the seventh.)

By now Mum is sitting slumped forwards, her head in her hands. Christelle and I look at each other anxiously, then back at Mum, then at a white-haired porter who's just appeared on the ward. 'All right, my sweethearts?' he calls out jollily.

The old ladies laugh as he wiggles his hips down the ward; Christelle takes a sip of water from the cup on her nightstand.

'So, now I know 'ow 'ilary Barnett got Mercedes's novel,' she says quietly, her eyes glued to Mum's bent head, 'I send 'im an anonymous letter to tell 'im I 'ave ze tape and to say I want £10,000. Zen I send 'im anozer letter to tell 'im where to leave ze money.'

Abruptly Mum straightens up.

'Why didn't you just confront him?' she says sharply. 'Why didn't you tell him to come clean?'

Christelle looks at her, all eyebrows. 'Becoz I 'ear ze gossip about 'is wife disappearing! I do not want to disappear too!'

Mum explodes, 'For heaven's sake, Christelle! Felicity Barnett didn't disappear! She went to a New Age festival in Cornwall and never came back. She met a crystal healer, moved in with him, and is now living on the Isle of Wight!'

Ah!

Mum fumes on. 'Why didn't you go to the police? What possessed you to try blackmail?'

Christelle stares down at her lap. 'I waz desperate,' she mumbles. Her fingers are clenched tight. 'Desperate to move somewhere wizout so many of ze memories.' Her voice is shaking. 'I cannot afford anozer place by myself. Zat is why I ask for £10,000 — to put down ze deposit on a flat. I know if I go to ze police I will not get any money from ze book; Mercedes left no will. I know wiz-out ze money, I will never 'ave a chance to move on.'

Christelle is now crying quietly onto her hospital gown. Mum gets up and stares stony-faced towards the window. Then, melting, she says, 'Oh, come on, love,' and gives Christelle a hug. The porter, who is back with a wheelchair, takes one look at Christelle sobbing loud-ly into Mum's neck and says to me, 'Would a Polo mint help?' And when I say, 'No. Thanks,' he says, 'Right-oh,' and wiggles off.

After the comedy porter has gone, Mum sits up properly and looks Christelle in the eye.

'What you did was reckless and stupid,' she says, 'but it's not the end of the world. I'm sure if I talk to the police and tell them about the stress you've been under, they'll be sympathetic.'

At the thought of the police, Christelle's face goes whiter than an aspirin. Mum squeezes her hand.

'I know you don't want the authorities involved,' she says soothingly, 'but Hilary Barnett is clearly a desperate man. He's attacked you once and the sooner he's stopped . . . Look, I'm sure the police will be far more interested in prosecuting him than you; he's the one who's committed an assault.'

It takes a while for Christelle to realise Mum is right; miserably, she nods her head.

Mum carries on, 'How about Loz and I go by your

flat today, pick up the answerphone tape, drop it off at the police station and tell them you want to talk. That'll count in your favour. Then you can tell them in your own words who it was that broke into your flat and attacked you.'

'But how do you know Hilary hasn't already found the tape?' I burst out.

Christelle looks at me, her eyes like a cat's.

'He won't 'ave,' she says. The ghost of a smile. 'I sewed eet in ze top of my bedroom curtains, between ze linings. He would never zink to look zere.'

Soon, a nurse with a really groovy nose piercing trundles up with a trolley of bandages and announces that it's time for a change of dressing.

Mum gets to her feet and kisses Christelle on the cheek.

'I'll pop back later to see you with Karen,' she says, smiling.

And I think: Holy Moley! As if the poor woman hasn't suffered enough.

* * *

Back in the car, Mum gives me one of her squinty sideways looks. Straightaway I tell her how slim she's looking but, typical, typical, she's having none of it – and so, the interrogation begins.

'How did you discover Christelle was blackmailing Mr Barnett?' she asks, starting up the engine.

Be cool, Loz, I tell myself. Keep it simple. Don't say more than you have to.

'I found the blackmail note.'

'Where?'

'In the pile of new price lists Lucy asked me to post.'

'Hmm! And how did you know it was a blackmail note?'

'I read it.'

So far, so cool.

'But how did you know to read it?'

'What do you mean?'

'Did it, for example, say on the envelope, Blackmail Note Enclosed?'

Silence.

'Loz?'

More silence.

'Hmmm?'

Bugger!

'I said, did it say on the . . .'

'ALL RIGHT, ALL RIGHT! I opened it coz I thought it might be something lovey-dovey from you, OK?'

'I see. And why would I be writing something lovey-dovey to Hilary Barnett?'

'D'OH! Coz you're going out with him?'

'Since when?'

'I dunno! Since your date yesterday?'

'But I didn't have a date with Hilary Barnett yesterday.'

I blink at her. 'Huh?'

'What made you think I was on a date with him?'

'Man-mad Marge said he fancied you.'

'When?'

'At the party.'

'Oh, for heaven's sake, Loz! Since when have you paid any attention to what Marge says when she's had too much to drink?'

'But she said you were gonna ask him out.'

'Are you sure? Are you sure she didn't say *she* thought I should ask him out?'

'Er . . .' Now I come to think of it. 'But why would she have said that?'

'Because *she* wants me to ask him out.'

'Why?'

'To get me dating again. To get me interested in another man. To . . . help me get over your dad.'

There is a pause. One of those long, horrible ones. Then: 'But you did go to Babylon Lounge last night, right?'

'Yes, I did go to Babylon Lounge last night, but not with Hilary.'

'With who then?'

'You don't know him. His name's Dave. Dave Quick.'

Dave Quick?

'He's got a son at your school.'

WHAT? *Nooooooooooooooo!!!!!*

Just then Mum takes one of her heart attack turns into Hurlock Street and slams on the brakes outside Christelle's block. The car jumps to a stop like a kangaroo.

'Right,' she says, her face all smiles, like that last bombshell *never happened.* 'I shall look forward to hearing more about how you uncovered Christelle's blackmail scam after we've retrieved her answerphone tape.'

I open the door forcefully.

'By the way,' she continues, still smiling, 'did you remember to post the rest of the salon's price lists?'

The salon's price lists? Yikes!

'Yeah. 'Course. I did it yesterday.'

'Good, because I'd hate to think of you and Dex having to deliver all those envelopes by bike.'

I get out of the car and slam the door.

B-l-o-o-d-y Nora! Is there nothing Mrs Chief Inspector Nazi doesn't know?

★ ★ ★

By some miracle, Mum had remembered to bring Christelle's spare key with us to the hospital. She unlocks the front door and I follow her inside. The broken pane of glass near the lock has been boarded up, but the bloodstain on the lounge carpet is still there. Seeing the stain makes me feel a bit wobbly. From the look on Mum's face, it's not exactly making her feel steady either.

'Come on,' she says, shivering slightly, 'let's get this over and done with. It won't take a minute.'

And she's right. It doesn't take a minute. It takes *thirty-five*! First, we look for a stepladder to reach the top of Christelle's curtains only to discover there isn't one. Then we drag over the chest of drawers and Mum clambers up only to realise she hasn't got any scissors. Then I go into the kitchen and do a scissor search only to return empty-handed. Then Mum comes down and joins in the hunt until finally, finally, scissors in hand, she unpicks the answerphone tape while I nip to the bathroom for a pee. Honestly, talk about Operation Grease Lightning . . . Not!

As I'm sitting down on the toilet, I look round the tiny, white, window-less bathroom and think back to the last time I was here, looking for a towel, feeling desperate and frantic and scared.

And that's when I hear it: the unmistakable creak of a floorboard by the front door.

18

The Tape and the Tortoise

I yank up my knickers and stand behind the bathroom door, heart pounding. I hadn't closed it properly (nor the front door, it seems) so I can see a thin strip of hallway. Across it, Hilary Barnett is moving slowly. As he creeps forward, I spy Mum coming out of Christelle's bedroom, the answerphone tape in her hand. For a chilling moment she and Hilary say nothing, not a word. Then he croaks, 'Anne . . . I – I . . .' And Mum cuts him off.

'If it's the tape you're after,' she says coldly, 'you're too late.'

My feet are rooted to the spot. Panic is flooding my veins. *I don't know what to do!* I crack the door a tiny bit more and Mum's gaze flickers. I can't see Hilary's face because his back's to me, but I can see Mum's, and her eyes are *flaring*.

'How could you?' she says, her voice hard and low. 'How could you attack Christelle?'

He stammers, 'I – I didn't mean to. Christ knows I didn't mean to.' It's like he's pleading. 'I thought she was out at work. I didn't expect her to surprise me like that. I just panicked, hit out.'

'You left her unconscious.' Mum's face is rigid with rage.

'I panicked,' he gushes. 'I panicked. I was in shock. I didn't know what to do. I walked around and around.' The back of his neck is sweating. 'I was going to come back up, to get help, but then, when I got back to the block, I saw Lauren and Dexter going up the stairs to the flat and I thought . . .'

His voice trails off and with a groan of despair, he crouches down, like a toad, and drops his head in his hands.

For a moment, nothing happens. Nothing at all. Then Mum catches my eye and, fast as fast, without warning, Hilary lunges forward, grabs the answerphone tape from her hand and, spinning round, takes off for the open front door. Before he knows what's happening, I shove my foot out in front of him, and he flies through the air and slams to the ground, *thud*, like a sack of bricks. As he lands – half in, half out of the door – Mum lets out this awesome warrior cry and hurls herself on top of him. Hilary struggles, like a man possessed, and I jump on his legs.

'Nice work, Loz,' puffs Mum, clinging on like a rock climber.

By now doors are opening along the concrete walk-way; someone is yelling, 'Call the police.' A tattooed bloke with arms the size of boulders shouts out, 'What's going on?' and when Mum shouts back, 'I'm making a citizen's arrest,' he lumbers forward and sits on Hilary's head.

YEEEEEESSSSSSSSSSS!!!!!!!!

The three of us are still sitting on Mr Barnett when the police show up.

★ ★ ★

After the arrest, me and Mum tell the police everything we know. Which is a lot! Then we stop off at the China Garden for a blow-out meal and a blow-by-blow review of our spectacular takedown. And it *was* spectacular. You should have seen Mum's flying tackle! After that Mum drops me home before skipping off to check the salon hasn't burnt down or anything. And I mooch into the lounge, switch on the TV and flick through the channels:

BBC 1: Cricket. (B*ooo*ring.)
BBC 2: Horse racing. (No.)
ITV 1: A wildlife documentary about reptiles. (Maybe.)
Channel 4: *The Simpsons.* (Superb.)

I turn up the volume and am just snuggling down on the sofa with Mum's big white fluffy cushion clutched to my chest when, *Ping*, my brain makes the link: Reptiles. Tortoises. *Tortoises!*

I haven't quizzed Dad about his tortoises!

Quick as a wotsit, I shoot off the sofa and into the hallway, to the phone. I punch in Dad's mobile number and wait. I know he's probably out on a job right now, but he should still pick up. He does.

'Dad!'

'Loz! I was going to send you a text.'

'What's all this with you and tortoises?'

'Ah!' There is a bit of a silence. Then he says, 'Listen, love, I can't really talk right now; I'm behind with this job I'm on, then I've got that mobile phone mast meeting I was telling you about, then I'm seeing Steve in the pub. What I was going to text you to say was: Come round tomorrow. You can ask me whatever you like then.'

I frown. 'What time tomorrow?'

'I'll send you a text from the pub.'

'Why can't you tell me now?'

He laughs. 'All will be revealed tomorrow. What do you say?'

Grumpily, I say, 'All right.' (Hey, what other choice do I have?) And the next morning (Sunday) I set off for his flat at eleven o'clock, as agreed by text, but not before Tasha has come round to help me decide on an outfit for my date on Monday. After loads of trying on, we agree: my short, blue denim skirt; my new, flat, knee-high boots; my olive green vest, which isn't *tight* tight, but is as tight as I've got, and Karen's hooped earrings. (I had thought of wearing my favourite jeans but Tasha said, 'Best not, not with your bum.')

My date outfit sorted – finally – I say *au revoir* to Tasha and her 'tiny' bottom then go get my copy of *Rebel* to read on the bus to Dad's. As I open my school bag I let out a gasp.

Note to brain! Post the salon's price lists *today*.

Red alert sent, I dig through the envelopes until I find my mag, which is packed with the usual educational stuff. On page seven, there's the story of this girl who persuaded her boyfriend to murder her sister. And on page twelve, it says you can suss out a boy's personality by looking at the shape of his face. Apparently, if he's got a round face, he's the lazy type who prefers to be a follower than a leader. If he's got a rectangular face, like Dex, he's the honest type who finds it easy to make friends. And if he's got a square face, like Lee, he's the strong, silent type who prefers action to words.

Gulp!

I'm still thinking about Lee and his strong, silent actions when I reach Dad's block. I lean on his bell, he buzzes me in, and as I reach the first-floor landing, I think: Loz, you moron! Why didn't you get Dad to bodyguard you from the bus stop? I give myself a mental slap on the forehead, and am just about to charge up the second flight of stairs when this happens: there's a buzz from the front door below, then the sound of a door being flung open above, then the staircase shakes.

Thump! Thump! Thump!

I freeze to the spot.

Thump! Thump! Thump!

The shuddering is getting closer.

Two possibilities race through my mind. Either:

1. East Sussex is in the grip of a major earthquake or
2. I am very, very dead.

I stare up like an idiot at the familiar hulk thundering down towards me.

Oh, Nelly!

That's it!

I'm dead!

19

Mission Incredible

As Tonya's great hulk comes crashing downstairs towards me, I scream the loudest scream of my life, shrink back against the landing wall and fling my arms up over my head. My heart is smashing around my rib cage like a ball in a squash court. My brain is shrieking, *Oh God, help me, oh help me, help!*

But Tonya doesn't jerk back her fist. She doesn't kick forward her leg. She simply looks at me as if to say, *Freak*, and thunders on downwards — *thump, thump, thump* — down to the bottom of the stairs.

For a moment, my whole body stays totally rigid. Then I let out my breath and crumple into a heap.

I cannot believe what has just happened! *I cannot believe it!* Why didn't she head-butt me from here to hospital? How come I'm not on my way, right now, to intensive care?

On rubbery legs, I stagger across the landing and peer over the handrail. At the front door, Tonya is talking to someone I recognise: Dad's mate, Steve, who works for *The Echo*.

He says, 'Ready then?'

She says, 'You gotta go up the fire escape at the back to get to the roof. I'll show you.'

And with that, they turn right outside the main door and, *pooof!*, they're gone.

Two seconds later, the staircase is juddering again. This time the thudding is coming from a pale blonde woman the size of a combine harvester (Mrs Ravonia, I'm guessing) followed by another women who is going, 'Tracey, did I close my front door? I can't remember closing my door.'

Confused (very), I watch as these two turn right outside the main door, then I leg it up the stairs to the top and charge across the landing to Dad's. As I go to press his bell, the door flies open and a hand yanks me inside.

'Quick!' he hisses, still yanking. 'We haven't much time!'

And before I can shout, Time for what? he shoots down the hallway, through the lounge and out on to the balcony with me flapping along behind.

On the floor in the lounge, there's a huge wooden crate with five tortoises inside it, all different sizes and all with the words *Speedy Gonzalez* painted in white on the shell. Out on the balcony, there's a crane-like contraption with a metal claw dangling from a short cable. The claw looks like one of those mechanical grabbers down the arcade that Dex can never get to pick up the cuddly toy.

I open my mouth to speak – can you wonder? – and Dad presses a finger to his lips.

'Push that button and keep your finger on it,' he whispers, pointing to a red button on the base of the crane.

Not having the faintest foggiest what's going on, I press the button and hold it down while the claw drops silently, like a spider on a thread, over the balcony's wall.

'Nearly,' whispers Dad, leaning over the wall. 'N-e-a-r-l-y . . . Stop!'

I let go of the button and the claw zaps back up . . . holding a small tortoise with *Speedy Gonzalez* painted in teeny tiny white letters on its shell.

'Now,' whispers Dad, catching the tortoise as it drops from the opening claw. 'Swop it for the largest one.'

I take the cutsie creature from his hands and dash into the lounge. As I'm picking the largest tortoise out of the crate, a shiver of excitement zips up and down my spine.

'Is this Tonya's tortoise?' I half whisper, coming back out.

Dad nods and that shivery thing happens again.

After that, me and Dad are like two agents from *Mission Impossible*: smooth, silent and slick.

1. I hold tortoise under claw. Dad pushes button. Claw grabs tortoise and drops to window box below.
2. I give signal. Dad releases button. Empty claw comes back up.
3. Dad signals to me to move crane sideways. (Hey, it's on wheels!) Crane can no longer be seen from ground.
4. Dad moves towards lounge and hits head on crane. The smooth, slick, silent thing is kippered completely.

'Let's go!' he shouts, rubbing his forehead with one hand and grabbing his mobile phone with the other.

And with that, he's off – me following – out of the flat, down the communal staircase, through the main front door, round the side of the block, and up the metal fire escape to the huge flat roof.

Once on the roof, Dad clutches his sides like he's just been skewered with a giant kebab stick, and I pant like a racing greyhound. Which is attractive . . . not. Up ahead of us, Steve is photographing Tonya – arms folded, face mean – next to the mobile phone mast. And Mrs Ravonia and the woman tenant are standing around, watching, interested.

'Right,' says Steve, pretending he hasn't seen us. 'Let's get a shot of you and your amazing shrunken pet.'

Like a puffer fish that's just won a puffing contest, Tonya swells with pride and thuds off down the fire escape to get her tortoise. Steve slips me a wink then turns to talk to Mrs R. I look up at Dad, eyebrows raised, and he grins like he did that time he gave me a plastic snake to put in Nan's bed.

'It all started last Sunday,' he says, voice hushed, 'after you'd told me about Tonya's threat. I was thinking about ways you could get back at her and I remembered that Roald Dahl story I used to read to you when you were little, the one about the lovesick man who winched up his neighbour's tortoise from her balcony, to get her attention.

I grin, thinking: *Esio Trot*! I remember! I used to really adore that book.

Dad carries on, 'I asked Matt from the garage to help

me build the crane. Basically, it's a hydraulic machine with the master cylinder in the . . .'

I interrupt, 'Dad?'

'Yes?'

'No science.'

He closes his eyes and shakes his head as if to say, Where did I go wrong? Then he carries on.

'Each day we've been replacing Tonya's tortoise with a slightly smaller one so that she'd think her pet was shrinking.'

I burst out, 'That's genius!'

He grins. 'The hard part was the name painting. You've no idea how long it took to get my hand steady enough to paint *Speedy Gonzalez* in letters the size of an ant.'

I laugh. 'But what I don't get is, why did you do it? What for?'

'Hold on, I'm getting to that. A couple of days ago, I knocked on the Ravonias' front door to say I'd noticed their tortoise seemed to be getting smaller and had they considered that radiation from the phone mast might be the cause, and mightn't it be a good idea to bring this up at the mobile phone mast meeting.'

I practically hop up and down. 'Excellent!'

'I knew Tracey . . .'

'Who?'

'Mrs Ravonia.'

'Oh, yeah.'

'I knew she would jump at the chance of having her tortoise tale in the paper. So last night at the meeting, I introduced her to Steve who was covering the mobile phone mast story for *The Echo*. He owes me a favour so he agreed to play along and, as a result, he fixed up this fake photo-shoot with Tonya today.'

I gaze up at Dad in total admiration. He really is the world's greatest dad, as his T-shirt says.

Just then there's the slow sound of heffalump footsteps on the fire escape. Quick as a wotsit, Dad thrusts his mobile into my hand.

'You might want to video this,' he whispers.

And I switch the phone to film just as Tonya reappears, carrying what can only be described as a bloody huge tortoise. Like a zombie, with arms outstretched, she walks towards her mum and the two of them look at each other in shock and disbelief. Mrs Tenant looks in disbelief too. Then Steve starts to yell.

'What do you think you're playing at, girl?' he shouts. 'This tortoise is the size of a tank!'

Tonya splutters, 'But it was really small this morning. Honest. You saw it, Mum. Tell him how small it was.'

Steve looks ready to burst a blood vessel. 'It was small this morning, but it's full-size now? What do you take me for? An imbecile?'

'But . . .'

'I don't want to hear it!'

'But . . .'

'I said I don't want to know! You've wasted enough of my time already.'

Tonya's face is as red as a raspberry. Her mum's, as white as milk.

'Are you getting this?' says Dad out of the corner of his mouth. I nod, beaming. 'Good, because I'm sure your class would be keen to see it should Tonya ever try to carry out her threat.'

For a second I stare at Dad, not sure I've heard him right. Then, suddenly, my heart swells like a balloon. I can't believe it! My very own blackmail weapon! Oh! Oh! How *brilliant* is that?

By now Steve is packing up his camera equipment huffily; Mrs Tenant is shaking her head.

'But it was shrinking!' stomps Tonya to no one in particular. 'It was! It was!'

Furious, furious, practically spitting with fury, she looks over at Dad for some kind of backup, and I give a little wave . . . with my phone-filming hand.

That does it. Her jaw hits the floor, the blood drains from her face, and she makes a strange choking sound like she's just swallowed some soap.

YEEEEEEEEEEEEEEEESSSSSSSSSSSSS!

RESULT!

Even, at last.

20

Sorted

You don't need to be a genius to know that the whole world is talking about Hilary's arrest, because the second me and Dex get into school on Monday practically everyone in the grounds either looks at me or rushes up to ask, 'Is it true? *Has* Mr Barnett been arrested?' (I nod yes). 'Is he being held in police custody?' (I nod again). 'Did he really murder his wife and bury her body up on the Downs?' (I say, 'Yes. Definitely. Absolutely.') Actually, there are so many questions, in the end I have to pretend I'm busting for the loo just so Dex and I can get away.

All through break the questions keep coming. And again later in the cafeteria with the gang. When, at last, the interrogation eases up, Tasha sits back in her chair, arms folded, lips pursed.

'I always knew Hilary Barnett was evil,' she announces. 'And a perve. Remember that time we bumped into him in WHSmith's, Loz, and he couldn't take his eyes off my legs?'

I nod, although to be fair, a flock of nuns would've

stared at Tasha's legs that day; her skirt was the size of a belt.

Ems changes the subject.

'What I don't get,' she says, 'is why Christelle didn't just go to the police when she realised what Hilary had done.'

I explain, 'Coz that way no one would've got the money for the novel. Mercedes didn't leave a will and she didn't have any rellys so, officially, there was no one to pass the money on to. At least if the blackmail scam had worked, Christelle would've got *some* money for the book, which is what Mercedes would've wanted.'

Ems frowns and picks up the salt pot. As she twiddles it up and down, the top drops off and salt pours into her lap.

'I still think Christelle should've gone to the police,' she mumbles, shaking out her skirt. 'That way Mercedes could've had her name put on the front cover.'

'Actually, that's what will happen now, according to Mum,' I reply. 'The novel will be withdrawn and reprinted with Mercedes's name on the front.'

'But what's gonna happen to Christelle?' cuts in Dex anxiously. 'She won't go to prison, will she?'

I shake my head. 'No. Mum says the police know a jury would be on her side so there wouldn't be much point in sending her to court.'

Dex sits back, relieved; Ems jumps in, 'So, do you think Hilary'll go to prison for long?'

Straightaway Nat says, 'For sure.'

I say, 'For definite.'

And Tasha adds, 'For life, hopefully.'

Ems looks shocked. 'Aw, c'mon, Tash. Don't be mean. I know what he did was really bad, but it isn't like he actually murdered anyone, is it?'

Tasha snorts. Ems always looks for the good in people: it's her most annoying habit. Tasha rarely does: that's hers.

Up until this point, Dex's been looking mega serious. Now he grins.

'Imagine,' he says, 'Hilary's face when he busted open your box and found that cassette of your Dad's band and played it, thinking it was Christelle's answerphone tape.'

I burst out laughing; Tasha interrupts.

'I didn't know your dad's in a band.'

'He isn't, but he was.'

'Were they famous?'

'Is Tonya a twig?'

'No. Oh, I see. Yeah.'

Good grief!

After lunch, Tasha, Dex and Nat dash off: Tasha to phone Gary; Dex to find Pete Ray; Nat to Old Retardo's office to explain why she'd advertised his car for sale in *The Echo*. Ems dashes off, too – to the toilet – leaving me to put my dirty tray in the rack. As I'm sliding it into the slot, I can feel someone at my back. I spin round and there, luscious as life, is Lee.

'So . . . what d'ya want to do tonight?' he asks, eyes sparkling.

'Er . . .' B-l-o-o-d-y Nora! 'Um . . .' I think my insides may have melted. 'Er . . .' Brain, get a grip! 'We could listen to music. Have a chat.'

He smiles lopsidedly. 'What about?'

'Oh, I don't know,' I say casually. 'The state of the ozone layer? Women's rights? World affairs?'

He looks at me like I've just sprouted a beard. Then, seeing the grin creeping up my face, he goes, 'Yeah. Right. World affairs. Nice one!' And we both laugh.

By now a crowd of his mates is approaching, making kissy, kissy noises.

'Gotta go,' he says, reluctantly. '*Chat* to you later, yeah?' And with that, he's gone.

For one mad moment I wonder whether I should race after him and tell him about his dad and my mum at the Babylon Lounge, but then I think, no, best not. I mean, suppose I run out of worldly affairs to discuss on our date? I might be glad to have something less global up my sleeve for discussion. Although it'd be better if it wasn't, 'Lee, how do you feel about becoming my half-brother?'

Obviously.